THE BRIDGE HOME

◆

THE
BRIDGE
HOME

Padma Venkatraman

 NANCY PAULSEN BOOKS

NANCY PAULSEN BOOKS
an imprint of Penguin Random House LLC, New York

Visit us online at penguinrandomhouse.com

Library of Congress Cataloging-in-Publication Data
Names: Venkatraman, Padma.
Title: The bridge home / Padma Venkatraman.
Description: New York, NY: Nancy Paulsen Books, 2019.
Summary: Four determined homeless children make
a life for themselves in Chennai, India.
Identifiers: LCCN 2018035686 |
ISBN 9781524738112 (hardback) | ISBN 9781524738129 (ebook)
Subjects: | CYAC: Homeless persons—Fiction. | Runaways—Fiction. | Chennai (India)—
Fiction. | India—Fiction. | BISAC: JUVENILE FICTION / Family / Siblings. | JUVENILE
FICTION / People & Places / Asia. | JUVENILE FICTION / Social Issues / Runaways.
Classification: LCC PZ7.V5578 Br 2019 | DDC [Fic]—dc23
LC record available at https://lccn.loc.gov/2018035686
Printed in the United States of America.
ISBN 9781524738112
5 7 9 10 8 6 4

Design by Jaclyn Reyes.
Text set in Adobe Garamond Pro.

To Margarita Engle,
with admiration, affection, and gratitude—
your generous support and steadfast encouragement
mean more than I can express

CONTENTS

GLOSSARY

◆

aamaam: yes

akka: older sister

amma: mother

appa: father

aunty: a term of respect used for older women; often used as part of their name

biryani: a spicy rice dish

Divali: a major Hindu holiday, the "festival of lights," that takes place in late October or November

Ganesha: a Hindu God with a man's body and an elephant's head, considered, among other things, a patron of wisdom and learning

gulab jamun: sweet, deep-fried balls made of a milk-based dough and soaked in rose-flavored syrup

illam: house or home

kolam: a decorative pattern made from rice flour sprinkled on the ground

kurta: a type of tunic

laddu: a round confection, usually served at celebrations and holidays

murukku: a crispy snack made of lentil flour shaped into spirals and deep fried

nadhaswaram: a double-reed wind instrument that sounds a little like a saxophone

paavum: poor thing

pakora: fritters made by dipping vegetables in batter and frying them

pavadai: a type of skirt

payasam: pudding made with rice or vermicelli-type noodles

rakshasi: a female demon

rasam: a spicy and watery sauce usually served over rice and often made with tomato and lentils

roti: Indian flatbread

rupee: the currency in India, worth much less than a dollar

sari: a traditional Indian dress consisting of a piece of cloth that is wrapped elegantly around the body

vadai: a type of lentil fritter

vanakkam: a greeting

1

—————◆—————

TOGETHERNESS

Talking to you was always easy, Rukku. But writing's hard.

"Write her a letter," Celina Aunty said, laying a sheet of paper on the desk. Paper remade from wilted, dirty, hopeless litter that had been rescued, scrubbed clean, and reshaped. Even the pencil she gave me was made from scraps.

"You really like saving things, don't you?" I said.

Crinkly lines softened her stern face. "I don't like giving up," she said.

She rested her dark hand, warm and heavy, on my shoulder.

"Why should I write?" I said. "It's not like you have her address."

"I believe your words will reach her," Celina Aunty said.

"We're opposites," I said. "You believe in everything and everybody. You're full of faith."

"Yes," she said. "But you're full, too. You're full of feelings you won't share and thoughts you won't voice."

She's right about that. I don't talk to anyone here any more than I have to. The only person I want to talk to is you, Rukku.

Maybe writing to you is the next best thing.

If you could read my words, what would you want me to tell you?

I suppose you'd like to hear the fairy tale you'd make me tell every night we huddled together on the ruined bridge. The story that began with *Once upon a time, two sisters ruled a magical land,* and ended with *Viji and Rukku, always together.*

That story was made up, of course.

Not that you'd care whether it was true or not. For you, things were real that the rest of us couldn't see or hear.

When I finished the story, you'd say, "Viji and Rukku together?"

"Always." I was confident.

Our togetherness was one of the few things I had faith in.

2

◆

ROTTEN FRUIT

You always felt like a younger sister, Rukku. You looked younger, too, with your wide eyes and snub nose. You spoke haltingly, and you hunched your shoulders, which made you seem smaller than me, though you were born a year before.

Born when our father was a nice man, I suppose, because Amma said he was nice. Before.

Imagining Appa "before" took a lot of imagining. I was a good imaginer, but even so, I couldn't imagine him all the way nice.

The best I could do was think of him as a not-yet-all-the-way-rotten fruit. A plump yellow mango with just a few ugly bruises.

I could imagine our mother picking him out, the way she'd pick fruit from the grocer's stall, choosing the overripe fruit he was happy to give her for free. I could see Amma looking Appa over, hoping that if certain foul bits could be cut away, then sweetness, pure sweetness, would be left behind.

Because Amma did choose him. Their marriage wasn't arranged.

Somehow he charmed her, charmed her away from her family, with whom she lost all touch. They were ashamed, she told me, ashamed and angry with her for eloping with someone from an even lower caste than the one she'd been born into.

It was all she ever said about her family. Not their names or where they lived or how many brothers and sisters she had. Only that they wanted nothing to do with us. And Appa's family—if he had one—didn't seem to know we existed either.

Sometimes I wonder if they might have helped us if they'd known. But maybe they'd have done nothing, or acted like our neighbors and schoolmates, who did worse than nothing. Who sniggered or made rude comments when we walked past. Comments that upset you so much, you stooped even lower than usual, so low it looked like you wanted to hide your head inside your chest.

———————

On my eleventh birthday, when we came home from school, I was surprised to see saucepans full of food simmering on the stove.

"Amma, you cooked!" I loved evenings when Amma felt strong enough to prepare dinner for us, instead of the other way around. "You even made payasam?" I inhaled the sweet scent of milk rice that wafted through our apartment.

"Not just that." Amma dug out a small money pouch from its hiding place, underneath the rice sack. "Here's two hundred rupees, for you to buy something for yourself."

"Two hundred rupees!" I was so astonished that I almost dropped the pouch before securing it to my ankle-length skirt.

"I've been saving a little of what Appa gives me for food and rent. I wanted to buy something, but I was too tired to go shopping for a gift, and I wasn't sure what you'd like."

"This is the best gift, Amma. Thanks."

"Sweet?" you said. "Sweets for Rukku?"

"Proper food first," Amma said. "For you both."

Amma heaped rice onto our plates and ladled some hot, spicy rasam over the top. She started eating, but you just stared at your food, your hands crossed over your chest.

"Come on, Rukku." I tried to feed you a spoonful of rice and rasam.

"No!" you yelled. "Sweet! Sweeeeer!"

"Don't get angry, Rukku. Please? Eat and I'll tell you a story tonight."

"Story?" You calmed down.

Amma looked at me gratefully.

We'd just finished our dinner when we heard Appa's heavy footsteps. The sound of him staggering up the stairs to our apartment told us all we needed to know.

"Get in your room. Quick," Amma said.

"Sweet," you moaned, but your hand met mine and we crept into our bedroom. In the darkness, we huddled together, unable to block out the sound of Appa yelling at Amma. We rocked back and forth, taking comfort in each other's warmth.

———————

Appa broke Amma's arm that night, before storming out of the house.

"I need to see a doctor," Amma came and told us. Her voice was tight with pain. "Stay with Rukku. If they see her—"

She didn't finish her sentence. She didn't need to. She'd told me a million times how scared she was that if you set foot in a hospital, the doctors might lock you away in "a mental institution."

You curled up on our mattress with your wooden doll, Marapachi. I smoothed your brow.

The patch of moonlight that slipped past the rusty iron bars on our window fell on the book that our teacher, Parvathi, had given me before she moved away. No other teacher had ever been so nice, even though I was often at the top of the class.

I opened the book. In a shaking voice, I read you a tale about a poor, low-caste girl who'd refused to accept the life others thought she should lead.

"You think we could change our lives, like that girl did?" I asked. "And Parvathi Teacher. And Subbu. Or at least his family. They all left for a better life in a big city."

Subbu had been the only friend we'd had in school. His long face and thin frame had made him look as weak as a blade of grass, but he'd always told off the other children who teased us.

"I miss him, Rukku. Think he ever misses us?"

You answered me with a snore.

I was glad you'd fallen asleep, but I stayed awake, worrying and hoping. I hoped Amma would finally tell someone about how she had been hurt, and that they'd swoop down and rescue us.

But I should have known she'd never tell.

3

❖

BREAKING

The next day, Amma pretended like nothing had happened.

You never pretended.

"Owwa," you announced. You patted our mother's good arm and stroked the sling on the broken one.

When Appa came home that evening, his eyes bloodshot and his breath reeking as usual, he set packages wrapped in newspaper on the cracked kitchen counter. "Presents for my girls."

"How nice!" Amma's voice was full of false cheer.

"Sorry I lost my temper last night." He placed a finger on her chin. "I'll never do it again. Promise."

I saw hope creep into Amma's eyes. Desperate, useless hope.

Suddenly, I wanted to shout at her, more than at him. *Have you forgotten how often he's broken his promises?*

He ripped open one of the packages and dangled a pair of

bangles in front of you. But before your fingers could close over them, he jerked them away.

"Catch!" He launched one bangle over your head, and as you slowly raised your hands to try to catch it, he sent the other flying so fast, it struck you before tinkling to the floor.

You squeaked like a trapped mouse.

He laughed.

How dare he think it was funny to trick you. How dare he mock your trust.

When he tossed a package in my direction, I didn't even try to catch it. I crossed my arms and watched it land on the floor.

"How bad both our girls are at catching!" Amma's voice was high-pitched and tense as a taut string.

"Stupid," he said. "One with slow hands, and the other with a slow brain."

"We're not stupid!" I picked up my package and flung it at him.

Nostrils flaring, he slapped me.

"Please," Amma begged. "Not the children."

You leaped and thrust your doll between me and Appa.

He kicked out at you.

At you.

Furious, I lunged at him. You joined in, and the two of us barreled into him together. He swayed and fell backward, but not before he struck your face.

Amma caught him, instead of letting him crack his head on the floor.

"Let them be," she pleaded.

Appa grunted.

I was sure he'd come at us again, but instead, he crawled into their bedroom and passed out for the night.

——————

You ran a finger around the edges of what felt like a painful bruise blooming on my cheek. "Owwa," you said, paying no attention to your own wound. "Poor Viji."

With her unbroken arm, Amma grabbed a towel. She dipped it into the cool water in our earthen pot and pressed it against your bleeding lip. You struggled until I promised it would help you heal.

"Leave Appa," I told Amma. "Let's go somewhere else."

"How would we live, Viji?"

"We'll find a way."

"We can't manage without him. No one employs uneducated women with no skills." Her voice was flat. Defeated. "Just don't talk back anymore, Viji. I couldn't stand it if he hurt you again."

"He hurts you all the time," I said. "And now that he's started on us, nothing's going to stop him."

She didn't argue. Her head drooped, and when she finally found the strength to lift her eyes to mine, I could see she knew what I'd said was true.

"I can't bear seeing you hurt, but how can I stop him?" She gazed at the pictures of the Gods and Goddesses smiling down serenely from our kitchen wall. As if they'd suddenly leap into life and start helping.

"Please understand, Viji." She was begging me, the same pathetic way she'd begged Appa. "I promised . . . to be a good wife . . . no matter what. I can't leave."

But after what he'd done to you, I couldn't stay.

As I gazed at Amma's trembling chin, I realized how different we were. Amma trusted that if she put up with things, she'd be rewarded with another, better life after she died. It made no sense to me why any God who made us suffer in this life would start caring for us in the next.

If I wanted a better future, I needed to change the life we had. Now.

The more I thought about our differences, the surer I felt that I could protect you better than she could. She hadn't tried to stop Appa from beating us. All she'd done was beg. I would never become like her, I promised myself. I'd never beg anyone for anything.

———————

At the first light of dawn, while Amma and Appa slept, I woke and changed into my best blouse and ankle-length pavadai as silently as I could. Around my waist, I tied the drawstring purse with Amma's gift of money. Then I crammed a sheet, some towels, and a change of clothes for each of us into our school backpacks. I added a bar of soap, a comb, and the pink plastic jar of tooth powder to your bag; from the kitchen, I grabbed a bunch of bananas—your favorite fruit—to add to mine.

Our bags were heavy, but I couldn't bear to leave behind the book from Parvathi Teacher. Carrying it along was like taking her blessings with us, I told myself as I forced it into my bag.

Then I woke you.

"Shhup. Don't say a word, Rukku, please. Just get changed. We're leaving."

Sleep weighed down your eyelids, but you did as I asked. Perhaps it felt like a dream to you.

As we shuffled toward the front door, you cast a bewildered glance at our parents' bedroom.

"Amma?" you said.

Memories of our rare happy moments gleamed in my mind, like sunshine slipping into a dark room: the day Amma had helped you make a bead necklace, the night she'd sat by our beds and listened to the story I'd told you.

For a moment I hesitated. But then I glanced at your cut lip—the proof Appa had given me that he'd keep on hurting you as long as you were nearby.

We had to leave, right away, before fear or doubt slowed me down.

4

◆

ESCAPE

You followed me unquestioningly until I turned down a different road, away from our usual route to school.

"School?"

"No, Rukku. We're going to a new place. A nicer place."

"Nicer place?"

"Far from here. You and me."

"Rukku and Viji together?" You offered me your soft, trusting hand.

With our fingers interlinked, I felt braver. I led the way to the main road, where buses to and from the city roared through our village.

In front of the bus stop sign, a woman was already waiting, chewing tobacco as placidly as a cow chewing its cud. A large basket filled with coconuts was beside her.

"Waiting for the bus to the city?" My voice trembled as I

checked to make sure we were in the right place.

"*Aamaam,*" she confirmed. Her eyes roved across my face, which was smarting with pain, and then settled on your cut lip, but she didn't comment.

Soon enough, a bus arrived, raising a cloud of red dust that made you sneeze. The woman balanced the coconut basket on her head and climbed in.

"Come, Rukku."

"No." You dug in your heels.

"Rukku, come!" I stepped into the bus.

"No, no, no," you sang out. "No."

The driver honked to hurry us.

"I'll give you a sweet." I tugged at you. "I'll give you a sweet when we're in the city."

You wriggled free of my grip.

"Get in or get out!" the driver yelled. "I can't wait all morning!"

The bus started to pull away.

I leaped out.

You jumped in.

"Vijiiiiii!" You leaned halfway out of the bus.

Horrified, I raced behind it.

I'd never have caught up to that bus if it hadn't been for the conductor's shrill whistle, calling the driver to a stop.

I climbed in, squishing down my sudden urge to haul you off the bus and run home.

The conductor helped me lead you down the aisle.

"Sweet?" You settled into a seat, and I slid in beside you.

"Not yet." I tried to catch my breath. "Don't have any sweets, Rukku."

The conductor looked at me and then at you, and stuck a hand in his pocket and pulled out a hard green sweet that had melted out of shape.

Green was your favorite color. You gave him a lopsided grin.

"Thanks," I said. "You're very kind, sir."

"No need for thanks. Going to the city?"

"Yes, sir."

He handed me our tickets.

My hand was shaking as I opened the drawstring purse at my waist, partly because I was nervous, partly from shock at how high the fare was. The tickets used up most of our money.

You unwrapped the sweet, popped it in your mouth, and stared at the green rice fields that flashed past the window. I wondered if you understood we were leaving forever. I was never sure what the words *yesterday* and *tomorrow* meant to you. Your sense of time was different from mine.

"Marapachi?" You rummaged in your bag, pulled out your wooden doll, and talked to her for a while. Then you stuck her back in your bag and slumped against my shoulder. The motion of the bus soon made your eyelids droop.

While you slept, doubts slithered into my mind. Had I done the right thing? Where would we go, once we reached the city? How would we survive?

5

◆

SHARDS OF GLASS

You jerked awake as the bus thudded to a halt. "We're here," I said, trying to sound cheerful.

The open-air bus terminal was packed with people shouting, laughing, and arguing. The smell of ripe guavas, piled high on a handcart pushed by a vendor, mixed with the smell of diesel smoke from buses. You held Marapachi close to your chest and stroked her wooden head.

As I wondered which way to go, I heard a voice right behind us. "There you girls are."

I whipped around.

It was the bus driver. He'd crept so close behind that I could feel his hot, foul-smelling breath on my neck. "You girls need a job? Money? I'll show you around the city."

I didn't dare answer.

"What's her name?" He jerked a thumb at you.

For once, I was relieved he hadn't asked you directly. You weren't as suspicious of people as I was, and the last thing we needed was to strike up a conversation with him.

I quickened our pace, but he kept up.

"Come with me." His hand came down on my arm and formed a vise.

"Let go!" I struggled. "Let go!"

A few bystanders glanced our way, but no one tried to stop him.

I tried to kick his shin—and missed.

"Don't you dare, you filthy low-caste brat!" He twisted my arm so hard, I gasped.

"No," I heard you cry. "No!"

Your arm swung back, and with all your might, you flung your hard wooden doll at him.

Marapachi hit his forehead with a satisfying thwack. He cursed, his grasp loosening enough for me to wrench free.

We raced away, deeper and deeper into the safety of the crowd.

———

When I finally felt safe enough to risk a look back, the bus driver was lost to my sight. Still, I decided we'd be better off if we crossed the road outside the terminal, putting as much distance between us as possible.

We waited for a break in traffic. And waited.

I'd never seen such an endless flood of vehicles and pedestrians.

Other people were darting in and out of the traffic, disregarding the deafening horns. Somehow they weren't getting run over. Holding you close, I stepped into the gap between a three-wheeled rickshaw and a motorbike. The motorbike almost ran over my toes.

"No, no, no!" You held my hand in a crushing grip.

"Move!" someone behind us snarled.

I heard the unlikely tinkle of a cow's bell. A great white cow was fording through the river of traffic, vehicles parting to let it through.

"Good cow." You put your hand on the beast's side as though you owned it. It didn't seem to mind.

Protected by the cow's bulk, we managed to reach the other side of the street.

"Good cow." You ran your hands along its neck.

"Yes, it's a good cow, but that bus driver was bad, Rukku. We've got to keep moving."

We came to a slightly less busy side street. On either side were run-down buildings that reminded me of our apartment. Towels, underwear, and faded saris flapped on clotheslines hung across the balconies.

Turning the corner, we found ourselves on an even narrower street, lined with shacks selling food. In one of them, a man stood behind a rickety counter. You watched, fascinated, as he poured steaming tea from one glass tumbler into another, until a layer of froth bubbled across the rim.

"We deserve a treat," I said. "How about sweet, milky tea instead of the sweet I promised you?"

"Tea," you agreed.

I was worried about how little money we had left, so I ordered us just one to share. As it warmed my hands and bubbles of froth tickled my lips, I knew it was worth the price.

I sipped slowly, then held it out to you. "Careful, Rukku. It's hot."

But before you could wrap your fingers around the slippery glass, I accidentally let go. You squealed, "Ai-ai-yo!"

Horrified, I watched the glass shatter on the ground, spattering tea across the hems of our skirts.

"Pretty." You reached down for a sparkly shard of glass.

"Don't touch!" I grabbed your hands. "It's sharp, Rukku! It'll give you an owwa!"

"Owwa," you echoed sulkily.

The teashop owner scowled at us. "Do you know how much that glass cost?" he asked.

Not that much, I was sure, but just before I opened my mouth to apologize, an idea struck me.

"Sir?" I offered. "We'll work to pay for the broken glass."

"Okay. Clean up the mess." The teashop owner stuck his hands on his hips. "Then go to the kitchen and help my wife."

"Yes, sir," I said.

"Viji?" You sounded uncertain.

"Everything's fine, Rukku." I gave you a quick hug. "We've found our first job."

6

◆

TEASHOP

The smell of roasting chillis tickled my nose as we ducked through the narrow doorway into the tiny kitchen at the back of the teashop.

A woman in a wrinkled gray sari turned away from the stove and looked at us. Her body was all sharp angles, but there was a softness in her eyes.

"We broke a glass," I explained. "We're working to pay it off."

The woman mopped her sweaty face with the free end of her sari.

"You'll help wash up?" she asked instead of ordering.

"Yes, ma'am."

"Call me aunty," she invited, with a quick smile. "Not rich enough to be called ma'am." She motioned at a stack of dirty glasses and plates.

I set our bags down beneath a shelf on which I saw a plastic image of Lakshmi, the Goddess of wealth, seated on a pink lotus. Though it was clear that the Goddess hadn't yet showered the teashop couple with riches, she was well looked after: a fresh jasmine garland was tucked across the picture, and a lighted incense stick was placed beneath it. Next to the Goddess was a picture of a young girl who had Aunty's eyes—whose photograph was also decorated with a jasmine garland.

I walked to the kitchen sink, but Teashop Aunty said, "No running water this time of day. Use the pail." Below the sink, I saw a green plastic bucket filled with water. There was a bit of coconut husk that I could use to scrape the dishes clean, and a tin of powdered soap.

"Don't use too much," she said. "Or he'll be shouting at us."

I liked that she said *us*, though she didn't even know my name yet.

"And we only have one more bucket of water. No more running water until four A.M. tomorrow."

"I thought in the city, people could get water from the tap whenever they wanted," I said.

"The city is the worst place," she said. "But my husband wants to live here, so what can I do?" She jerked her chin at you. "Your sister?"

"Yes. I'm Viji, and this is my sister, Rukku."

"Poor thing." She looked at you with pitying eyes—which I didn't like. But I kept my mouth shut. It could have been worse. She could have called you names and then I'd have started boiling inside like the oil in her frying pan.

"You come from where?"

I rinsed off a glass.

"Ran away?" she asked.

"Yes." There was no point trying to hide it. Our story was clearly written on my swollen face and your cut lip—but I didn't want to tell her the details and risk her feeling even sorrier for us.

Smoke billowed up from the hot oil, and Teashop Aunty turned back to the stove. She rolled some vadai dough into a ball.

Before she could do much more, you came over, pinched off another bit of dough, and rolled it between your palms, just as she was doing.

"She can do that quite well!" Teashop Aunty sounded amazed.

"Rukku's made vadais before." I tried not to let her surprise annoy me. Even the teachers at school—except for Parvathi Teacher—never bothered to find out how much you could do; Amma didn't really know either. "She's good with her hands. And she loves making bead necklaces."

"Rukku likes beads." You flattened the ball into a perfect circle, concentrating, with the tip of your tongue between your lips. "Rukku is a good helper."

"Ah! Very nice!" Teashop Aunty said.

I returned to the dishes as you helped her with the dough.

You started humming tunelessly as you worked. Homesickness pinched my heart for a moment. I thought of the rare weekends when Appa was away and Amma had enough energy to join us so we could cook a meal together.

By the time I was done with the washing, my hands felt raw, but the dishes were clean, and the teashop man grumpily agreed I'd done more than enough.

"You'll be all right?" Teashop Aunty asked, keeping her voice low so that the teashop man wouldn't hear.

"We'll be fine," I said.

Looking relieved, Teashop Aunty pressed two large bananas into your hands and a few vadais, hastily wrapped in a banana leaf, into mine. Then she let us out through the back door, into a lonely alley littered with plastic bags and broken bottles.

7

LOST PUPPY

Dusk was beginning to fall as we wandered out into the narrow street. My courage fell, too, with every step.

Fingering what was left of our money, I wondered how long it would last us. I regretted being too proud to share our story with Teashop Aunty. I should have asked her for help with finding a safe place to stay.

"Find Marapachi," you demanded.

"She's gone," I said. "You threw her at the bad man, remember?"

"Marapachi," you repeated, louder.

"You saved me, Rukku. You were a hero."

"Marapachi!" you yelled.

"We have better things to worry about than your doll," I burst out.

"Amma!" You turned your back to me. "Amma!"

"She's not here either. We just have each other now."

You plopped down, right there on the dusty street.

"Fine. Sit."

"Rukku wants Amma! Rukku wants Marapachi!"

"Shouting's not going to bring them here."

You scowled at me, and I spun on my heel and strode away, hoping you'd follow, but you didn't. I waited at the end of the street for a while, but you seemed quite content to stay where you were.

You won that round.

When I came back for you, you were bending over a skinny puppy with huge dark eyes.

"Get away from that puppy, Rukku. It might bite."

At the sound of my voice, the puppy thumped its tail. You stroked it tenderly, with just one finger.

"Come on. Please?" I said.

You started humming to the puppy. It licked you with its pink tongue.

"I'm really sorry, Rukku."

You made no move to show me you'd heard, though you usually forgave me if I sounded apologetic.

I crouched beside you.

The puppy looked right at me, and his nose crinkled, like he was smiling.

I couldn't help petting him. His coat was smooth. He wiggled and sniffed my hand.

"Rukku's dog."

I sighed. "We don't have enough to eat or a proper place to sleep yet, and you want to adopt this orphan?"

"Kutti," you announced, tapping his head. "Kutti."

"Kutti? That's what we're calling him?"

I knew there was no point trying to get you to leave the puppy behind. And I didn't want to leave Kutti behind either.

Because he'd smiled at me. And because he made you so happy. Your eyes were as shiny as the puppy's wet nose.

"Okay," I said. "But now we need to find a place to sleep."

"Come." You stood and beckoned to the puppy. "Come, Kutti."

Kutti pricked up his ears and stood attentively at your side, like he understood you perfectly.

"I have no idea where to go," I admitted. "You choose."

You broke into the widest grin I'd ever seen and started marching down the street. Realizing with a twinge of guilt that I'd never let you lead before, I followed.

On one street corner, three boys had already settled in for the night, huddled together on a tattered straw mat behind a dumpster. We saw another group of kids still at work, trying to sell newspapers to people who were stopped in their cars at a traffic light.

It felt good to have Kutti trotting close to our heels along the dark streets. He was probably too small to scare away strangers, but surely he'd bark in warning if someone tried to sneak up on us when we went to sleep.

If we ever found a place to sleep.

We walked beneath a huge billboard with a larger-than-life picture of a woman decked in gold jewelry—not just bangles and necklaces and earrings and nose rings, but even golden hair clips.

"Pretty," you said, pausing beneath it. "Pretty?"

GOLD AT SUPER-LOW PRICES AT THANGAM HOUSE, the billboard proclaimed—though the price for the necklace it advertised was a number followed by more zeros than I cared to count. "What comes after the ten thousands, Rukku?"

"Eleven," you said promptly. "Ten, eleven."

"Right." I smiled. "After ten is eleven, and we'll never have tens of thousands of rupees, so who cares what comes next?"

We wandered onto a wider road that led to a river. Two bridges spanned it—one was well lit with traffic rumbling across it; the other was dark and deserted.

We headed to the deserted bridge. Concrete lions stood on either side of what must have once been the grand entrance, and a crumbling concrete wall ran along its sides. The perfect spot to stay overnight, I decided. Probably the most secluded spot we could get in this city.

"Careful," I warned as we picked our way around the holes in the ruined bridge.

"Pretty." You pointed at the river that glittered like crushed glass far below us.

Halfway across the bridge, I saw a makeshift shelter. Someone had made a tent with a tarpaulin. Rocks held one edge of the tarpaulin in place along the wall of the bridge. The tent sloped down to the ground, where its other edge was held down with an old car tire. A cleverly built home, with one wall, a sloping roof, and two entrances.

"Looks like it was abandoned ages ago," I said. "Want to stay here?"

"Rukku wants to eat." You gobbled the bananas, and Kutti and I finished off the vadais.

Our food was gone before I realized I should have saved something for the next day.

It was beginning to get dark, but I could make out a boy marching up the bridge. He reminded me of a sunflower. Matted hair that looked like it had never met a comb stuck out like petals around a face that seemed much too large for his skinny body. He wore an oversize yellow T-shirt and a raggedy pair of shorts and held a bag and a wooden stick.

"*Vanakkam*," I greeted him, relieved that he was smaller than us.

"Go away," he said, instead of echoing *vanakkam* in return.

"You're polite, aren't you?" I said.

"If you stay here, my boss will come and . . ." He punched at the air. "Tishoom. Tishoom. He'll show you."

"Tishoom." You imitated him, repeating his nonsense word. "Tishoom. Tishoom."

He smiled at you.

Then he turned to me and said in a tone he seemed to think was impressive, "My boss is coming, with the rest of our gang."

"Your gang?" I peered into the gloom. No one else, as far as I could see.

"Ten—I mean, twenty boys, all ten times taller than me."

"You're a bad liar," I said.

"Owwa!" You pointed at a scab on his knee.

"Don't worry," he said to you, and he sat down cross-legged, pulling his T-shirt over his scraggy knees. "It doesn't hurt anymore."

Kutti sniffed at the boy and licked him.

"My name's Muthu," he said. "What's your dog called?"

"Rukku's dog," you said with pride. You sat right next to Muthu, as though he'd invited us to visit. "Kutti."

He patted Kutti tentatively. Then he glanced behind us. "Look! That's my boss."

8

ON A RUINED BRIDGE

A boy at least a head taller than me, though just as skinny as Muthu, was walking up the bridge. He had a wild mop of red-tinged black hair. A sack was slung across his shoulder, and he held a stick that was much sturdier and longer than Muthu's.

"Who are you?" the tall boy said.

"Who are you?" I said, drawing myself up to full height.

"I told you," Muthu said. "He's the big boss."

"What are you doing on our bridge?" the boy said.

"*Your* bridge? Why didn't you build a better one? Like that?" I pointed at the newer bridge.

Kutti trotted over, sniffed at the tall boy's bare feet, and then wagged his tail.

"Rukku." You gave the tall boy a warm grin and poked yourself in the ribs, then jabbed me. "Viji."

"I'm Arul." He flashed you a smile and then tried to look all stern. "We live here."

"So do we," I said.

"Get out," Arul said, so weakly that I guessed he was just putting on a show of protesting because Muthu was watching.

"We're already outside, in case you haven't noticed." I waved at the starry sky above, the twinkling river below. "And I don't need your permission to sleep here. It's not like you inherited this from your dad."

"Get your own tarp," he said. It was as good as a yes.

"You're going to let them stay, Arul?" Muthu said.

"We're staying." I gave him a smug smile. "No letting."

Arul tickled Kutti behind the ears and then disappeared into his tent. Muthu crawled in after him.

I found a relatively rubble-free patch of ground and spread out our sheet. Not that it made the ground any softer.

"Amma," you said, and looked all around us, as though our mother might pop out of the river and fly up through a hole in the bridge. "Amma?"

I put my arms around you, but you kept crying her name.

Kutti snuggled up to you, and you clutched one of his paws. He didn't seem to mind.

Hugging him close, like you used to hug your doll, you finally lay down on our sheet. "Story?"

Maybe hearing the familiar words would help take your mind off Amma. And my mind off the bumpy ground.

Not wanting the boys to overhear, I lowered my voice to a whisper. "Once upon a time, two sisters ruled a magical land."

"Viji and Rukku," you put in.

"Yes. Us. We used to be princesses, the two of us. We slept on soft pink pillows in a beautiful palace. Every morning, we'd wake to the sound of birds singing and the sight of peacocks dancing. White lotuses shone bright as stars in the lake at the center of our green garden. From this lake, a silver stream slipped out beyond our palace gates into the rest of our kingdom.

"No one in our kingdom was ever thirsty, because everyone could drink from that sparkling stream. And no one in our kingdom was cruel. Grown-ups never fought, and every child had all the dolls and toys they ever wanted."

"Dolls," you echoed. I was afraid you'd ask for Marapachi again, but you didn't start fussing.

"Every morning you made beautiful bead necklaces and I read you stories. We had hundreds and hundreds of books. Every afternoon we rode horses that could gallop so fast, we felt like we were flying."

Usually, I told you more about our horses or the wonderful fruits that grew in the orchard, but that evening I changed the story and added a new part. "One day, an angry demon cast a spell over our kingdom. Plants withered, birds stopped singing, and the stream dried up.

"The demon tried to catch us, but we ran away and found a place—this new place where he can't find us.

"We won't stay here forever. When we're older and stronger,

we'll leave. Together, we'll fight the demon, break his curse, and return to our lost kingdom, where we'll be princesses again. Viji and Rukku," I finished. "Always together."

"Viji and Rukku together?" you asked.

"Always."

"Viji and Rukku," you repeated. "Always together."

We had no roof or walls to keep us safe, and that probably should have worried me more, but you seemed content.

You pointed at the sky. "Look, Viji."

"No roof means we get the best view of the pretty stars, right, Rukku?" I said.

"Pretty," you agreed.

We lay shoulder to shoulder and watched the stars sparkle, while Kutti slept beside us. Your eyes sparkled, too, and the light inside them pierced through my fog of worry.

9

LAUGHTER

A cool breeze rose from the river, waking me and riffling the edges of my skirt. My stomach growled like a starving tiger. At home, the two of us would have been up, making breakfast. We'd been poor, but at least we always had something to eat.

When you woke, I knew you would be hungry, too. Maybe we could go to the teashop and ask if we could work there again.

Kutti woke with a snort. He snuffled at your face until you sat up.

"Amma?" you murmured.

"Just us, remember?"

"Go home now, Viji?"

"We live here now, Rukku. Our own place, like in our story."

"Palace?"

"Kind of. We rule ourselves here, so it's as good as being princesses."

You lifted your head high and surveyed the ruined bridge like a princess. Down by the riverbank, people were bathing. I spotted the boys by the river's edge.

From our bundle, I grabbed a change of clothes and our toiletries, towels, and water bottle. We walked down to the water with Kutti at our heels.

Up close the river was not beautiful. It looked more gray than silver.

We watched Arul dive off a rock, his heels kicking an old cardboard carton that bobbed past. With a joyful yip, Kutti splashed in, then ran back out to greet Muthu, who was still standing on the rock.

Muthu laughed as Kutti shook his coat, sending a shower of droplets into Muthu's face. "Now I don't need to wash," he said. "What a thoughtful dog you are."

"Good dog," you agreed. "Rukku's dog."

"Want to come for a swim?" Muthu grinned at you. "The water's nice and cool."

"No," I said. "Rukku can't swim."

"Let her have some fun!" Arul was wading to the shore. "We won't take her where it's deep."

Muthu cupped some water and let it dribble down your back. You giggled and slid into the river, with all your clothes on.

"Don't worry," Arul said. "We'll see that she's safe."

You splashed one another for a while, ignoring the litter that floated by. Kutti swam around you in circles.

If you hadn't been enjoying yourself so much, I would

probably have dragged you out. Part of me was irritated that you'd gone right ahead to bathe with the boys without me. But then, it was the first time I'd seen you make friends so easily. It was a nice change after years of meeting kids who hadn't been kind or warm to either of us—except for Subbu, whom Arul resembled a little.

"Want some soap?" I asked the boys.

"None for me," Muthu said. "I smell good enough already!" But Arul thanked me, and I waded into the water, and we started washing ourselves and the clothes we were wearing.

When we got out of the water, I gave the boys one of our towels, and Arul accepted it gratefully, though Muthu said he preferred to dry off in the sun.

Behind a bush, you and I peeled off our clothes and changed into the dry skirts and blouses I'd brought. With our fingers, we scrubbed tooth powder on our teeth and rinsed it off with the last of the water left in our plastic bottle.

———

Back at the bridge, I wrung out our wet clothes and towels, and weighted them down with stones to dry in the sun.

"Hungry," you announced.

"Sorry," I said. "Don't have anything. We'll go find something."

"No banana?"

"No, sorry."

"Papaya?" you suggested.

"No."

"Guava?"

"No. No pomegranate, no jackfruit, no oranges, no sapotes, no sweet limes. No nothing."

"No, no, no," you repeated, faster, louder, and more annoyed each time. "No, no, no!"

"No, no, no," Muthu joined in.

You stopped and stared at him.

"Let's sing together, Rukku," he said. "No-no-nooo!"

Kutti lifted his nose and let out a musical howl. "Wooo."

"Nooo!" You laughed and clapped your hands. "Nooo—nooo—nooo."

I'd seen you laugh before, but never quite like this. This was the first time you'd broken into a laugh halfway through a tantrum. And the first time you laughed without hiding your mouth behind your hands, as if you were scared to be happy.

Now you threw back your head the way Muthu was doing. And as the three of you howled away, like a pack of jackals, hungry and homeless though we were, I felt I'd done the right thing by leaving.

10

UNWELCOME

The city was waking up as we walked toward the teashop. Women were busy with their everyday routines, drawing kolams to decorate the ground before their houses.

At one home, you stood entranced as a woman showed a girl how to let rice flour fall evenly through her fingers to make the patterns with smooth white lines.

The teashop man was pouring frothy glasses of chai when we arrived. You wanted to walk right back to the kitchen, but I stood waiting for the man to notice me. If we showed him what polite, hardworking girls we were, surely he'd let us work for him again. Maybe pay us money this time.

"Go away!" he shouted.

I looked behind us to see whom he was shooing.

"You!" he yelled. "Get that dog away from my shop!"

"It's a good dog . . ." I began, but the man shook his fist at us.

Kutti growled. I picked him up and held his squirming body tight.

"Aunty!" you cried.

Sure enough, Teashop Aunty had opened the kitchen door a crack. She beckoned.

We took the long way around the shop, and I set Kutti down. He settled his head on his forepaws and closed his eyes.

Aunty let us in the back door with a slightly frightened smile. "You said Rukku liked beads?"

My irritation at her asking me instead of you vanished when she thrust a bulging bag into my hands. Inside the bag was a beautiful collection of jewel-toned beads, as well as some neatly knotted bundles of twine.

"Thanks," I breathed. "Look what Aunty gave us, Rukku."

You were as dazzled by the rainbow of color as I was. You settled down on the floor of the shack at once and started making a necklace.

"Viji, if you can watch the stove, maybe I could quickly show your sister some bead tricks?"

"Of course, Aunty."

She sat with you, showing you ways to tie pretty knots and braid strands together. Every now and then, she shot a worried look at the door, but the teashop man didn't bother us.

You were so happy, I felt reluctant to leave, but after a while, my worry took over, and I told you we had to go find a job.

I refilled our water bottle, and Teashop Aunty pressed a plastic bag with bananas and vadais into my hands.

"No, Aunty, you already gave us too much."

"Don't argue with your elders." She insisted on giving me something else—a raincoat. "Belonged to my daughter." Her eyes flickered across the picture of the young girl next to the picture of the Goddess. "Gave away most of her things when she died, but this was new—and—I—just couldn't part with it until now."

"Thanks, Aunty." I tried to squeeze all my gratitude into those two small words.

As we left, Teashop Aunty walked outside with us. "Try your luck there—it's where the rich people live." She pointed at a distant temple tower rising above the forest of buildings.

"Maybe someone will want a maid," she said. "But don't be too trusting. The world's not always a kind place for two poor girls like you."

The back alley wasn't as deserted as it had been the day before. A girl dressed in rags pawed at the hem of my skirt as we walked by.

"Give me something," she whined. "I have to look after my brother. See him?" She gestured at a small boy—stark naked—who was sleeping behind her.

Had they been runaways, too?

"*Kaasu kudunga, akka,*" she wailed. Give me some coins, sister.

"We don't have any money," I said. It was almost true.

"Money." You patted the money pouch at my waist.

I shouldn't have lied. You never did.

"We have no money to spare, Rukku."

Your eyes welled up as you gazed into the girl's tearstained face.

"Okay, okay." I untied the drawstrings, but before I could take a coin from the pouch, the girl's bony fingers clamped tight on it, and she yanked it out of my grasp. "No! That's everything we have!"

The girl scampered out of reach, her bare heels disappearing as she turned a corner, her brother forgotten.

Kutti yipped and darted after her, but I called him back.

Even if I'd felt less tired, I couldn't have chased a girl with such a pitiful voice and such haunting eyes. And besides, our money wouldn't have lasted much longer. We needed a job.

I looked for work in a few of the tiny shops we passed on our way to the temple—roadside shacks selling brightly colored clothes and cheap saris, fruit stalls humming with flies, a fragrant flower shop near the temple where two little girls sat weaving garlands of jasmine.

I saw more people that one day than I'd seen our whole lives. But nobody noticed us.

We were in plain sight.

But we were invisible.

11

◆

ORANGE

Sweat was rolling down our backs, plastering our blouses to our skin when we finally reached the temple. It was in a quiet part of the city, with tree-lined avenues and large houses surrounded by walls. One wall had bits of broken glass set into the concrete on the top, so no one could climb over without shredding their palms.

"Pretty," you said, reaching for the multicolored shards, through which sunlight skipped. "Pretty."

"No, Rukku! Owwa!"

Near the temple we found a house set in the middle of a sprawling garden. I could spot every kind of fruit tree—mango, coconut, banana, jackfruit, and even a short orange tree. The wall was low enough to look over, and it bore a sign with the house's name: LAKSHMI ILLAM.

"Look, Rukku. These people are so rich, they have time to

choose a name for their house!" I said. "They must want even more money, too, because they've named their house after the Goddess of wealth!"

Kutti ran up to the wrought-iron gate, which swung open invitingly.

Our feet crunched on the gravel path leading to the front door. We'd only taken a few steps when an old man picking oranges called out, "Ai! What do you think you're doing?" He looked us up and down, and I wished I'd smoothed our hair and skirts before entering the compound.

"I'm looking for work, sir, and—"

"Beggars?" He waved a fruit at us. "Get lost!"

"We're not begging," I said angrily. "I just told you I'm looking for work. I can do housework and—"

"You think rich people are going to give you jobs if you wander into their compounds with a mangy dog tagging along?" the old man said. "I'm the gardener here. Let me tell you what they'll do. They'll call the police, that's what!"

"Police?"

"Yes!" he said. "So keep out."

A noise came from a shed at the end of the driveway. To my surprise, a car drove out.

"House?" You pointed. "House? For cars?"

"That's called a garage," the gardener said.

The car pulled up to the front door of the mansion, and a woman in a sequin-studded sari stepped out. A girl in a lacy white dress skipped out from behind her.

"Look!" she cried. "What a cute doggie!"

"Get out." The gardener shook his fist at us, like he'd been trying to chase us away.

"Stay away from that dog, Praba," the woman said. "It's a stray."

I took your hand and walked briskly out the gate.

Something whizzed by my head. I ducked, shocked the gardener would go so far as to throw a stone just to keep up his pretense.

The object landed with a thud.

It wasn't a stone. It was an orange.

I looked back, wondering if I should thank him, but the gate clanged shut.

"Might as well eat it. It's not big enough to share with the boys," I mused.

You smiled.

We sat in the shade of a gnarled rain tree. Kutti settled his head on his forepaws and watched us.

I gave you the orange.

"Ahhh," you murmured, cradling it in your hands as if it were the most beautiful thing ever. You ran the tips of your fingers across its waxy peel. You turned it around and around, as if it looked different from every angle.

"Ahhh," you repeated. You raised the orange to your nose, took a long sniff, and then gave it to me.

I took the orange and turned it around, just as you had. It glowed like a small, pale sun.

I felt its weight, its perfect ripeness—not too soft, not too firm. I breathed in its citrus scent. I started to peel it, noticing things I'd never noticed before: how the leathery peel isn't colored the same all the way through, how the papery sections inside feel like leafy veins, how the pulp is shaped like raindrops.

When, at last, I placed a section in my mouth, I could hear it burst as my teeth met the flesh, squeezing the juice out onto my tongue, tart at first and then sweet. Everything else melted away except for the taste, the smell, the feel of the fruit on my tongue.

I ate the fruit slowly. The way you liked to do things.

Until then, I'd thought it was a sad thing that you were sometimes slower than the rest of us. But that day, I realized that slow can be better than fast. Like magic, you could stretch time out when we needed it, so that a moment felt endless. So the taste of half an orange could last and last.

12

CHOOSING FAMILY

By the end of that long day, I hadn't found a job. Our money was gone, and we weren't any richer, except for the raincoat and bananas and bag of beads that Teashop Aunty had given us.

Still, I felt thankful. Thankful we had at least that much. Most of all, thankful that you were following me without a fuss, with Kutti at your heels.

Smart, independent Kutti, who'd scampered off to eat scraps out of every open, overflowing garbage can we'd seen. We wouldn't have to worry about feeding him.

Arul and Muthu returned as we were trying to tie our raincoat to a steel rod that was poking out of the wall of the bridge to make a roof. Arms outstretched, you ran toward the boys.

The raincoat flapped in the wind and started flying about the bridge.

You squealed with excitement as I zigzagged after the raincoat, dodging the holes in the bridge. Kutti yipped and joined the chase.

"Cloth bird," Muthu yelled as he helped me catch it.

"Nice save." Arul clapped. "But that's not big enough for a roof."

"What do you know?" I huffed. "We don't need you telling us how to build a shelter."

"Too bad, because I got a spare tarp for you. A nice, big one."

"Now you tell me? After I almost twisted my ankle hopping all over the bridge?"

"You could thank me, you know," he said.

"I could," I agreed.

Arul grinned.

I grinned back.

"Well, maybe you'll want to thank me after we have some dinner."

We spread the raincoat on the ground and sat cross-legged in a circle around it. Arul set out their food—four crisp murukkus, wrapped in newspaper. My mouth watered, seeing the beige spirals made of spicy lentil flour.

I added the bananas that remained from the bunch that Teashop Aunty had given us.

Arul pressed his palms together and said a prayer I'd never heard before. It sounded like *our father, O. R. T. Narayan, something something*—all in English, not Tamil like Amma's prayers.

Then we split the food up evenly.

Almost.

Arul insisted he wasn't very hungry. He gave me his fruit to save for you for the next morning.

Ashamed that I was too selfish and hungry to be so noble, I downed my fair share.

After dinner, Arul helped us build our shelter. We tied one edge of the new tarp to the rods poking out of the wall of the bridge, right alongside their tarp. You and Muthu helped us stretch the other end of our tarp from the wall to the ground and weight down the bottom edge with stones to make a sloped roof. We hung our towel between the two sloped tarp roofs, like a wall. I spread out our sheet and bunched up the raincoat for you to have as a pillow.

"Sleep well in your new home," Arul said.

We crawled into our tent. I took out the book Parvathi Teacher had given me and strained my eyes, trying to read in the semidarkness, but I could hardly make out the words. I put the book away and thought of how kind she had been to us.

"When we grow up, I want to be a teacher," I told you. This dream had flitted through my mind before. Voicing it for the first time made my dream feel more solid. But it also made me worry if, by running away, I'd pushed it further out of my reach. "You think I can be a teacher someday? Subbu and Parvathi Teacher moved to cities so their lives could get better, right? Like us?"

"Story," you demanded.

I sighed. I didn't want Arul hearing my story and thinking it was silly, so I started whispering as I'd done the night before.

"Loud!" you commanded. "Palace! Peacock!"

"Okay, okay." I raised my voice a little and saw Muthu's shadow as he crept next to the towel dividing our tents.

When I was done, you demanded, "Again!"

I was about to protest when Muthu's voice floated through the thin barrier between us. "Yes, Akka, please? One more time?"

His words made my throat squeeze up, and it was a few moments before I could speak again.

He'd called me *akka*, older sister. He'd made me family.

13

WORK AND PRAY

That morning, after we'd combed our hair, I offered our comb to the boys. "If you'd like," I said hesitantly, not wanting to offend them, "you can use this . . ."

Muthu snickered. "Next you'll try to make us iron our clothes."

"Thanks." Arul stuck the comb in his tangled hair and yanked. "Months since I did this."

"Months, really?" Muthu said. "Akka would *never* have guessed that just by looking at your hair, boss."

The comb snapped in two.

"Tak!" You imitated the sound of the comb breaking and clapped your hands. "Tak! Tak! Tak!"

"Sorry," Arul said, tugging at the piece left in his hair. It stuck up at a jaunty angle, refusing to come out.

"Why are you sorry, boss?" Muthu pealed with laughter. "You just made two combs out of their one."

"Never mind," I said. "Here, let me help."

I pulled out the stubborn piece of comb, along with a chunk of Arul's hair.

He yelped and rubbed his head, but continued apologizing. "I feel bad. Is there anything I can do to make it up to you?"

"There is something you can do," I said. "You can promise to eat your share of our food every night."

"What do you care how much I eat?" Arul asked.

"I don't care. It's just that if you eat your fair share, then I won't have to feel guilty about doing it either. You made me feel like a greedy pig last night."

Arul grinned.

"It's silly to skip meals," I said. "How are you going to live a nice long life if you don't eat properly?"

"What's the point of living longer?"

"Well, what's the point of dying sooner?"

"I don't mind going off to meet our father who art in heaven as soon as I can."

"Our father who art in heaven? Oh, you said that last night. Your father is dead?"

"Yes. But I wasn't praying to *my* father," he said. "I was praying to God. He's called our father."

"God's our mother, too."

"Only if you're Hindu," he said. "Hindus have a million

names for God, but all are wrong, because Hindus worship the wrong Gods."

"I've never heard anyone say there's a right name or a wrong name—let alone a right God or a wrong God," I said. "Anyway, it doesn't matter to me, because I don't pray."

"You really never pray?" Arul looked horrified. "Even the wrong Gods are better than no God."

"My mother must've prayed a million times for our father to be better to us, but he only got worse. He always hit her, and then one night he beat us, so we ran away." I cast a glance at you, wondering if it would upset you to hear me talking about Appa, but you and Muthu were busy combing Kutti's scanty fur with one of the pieces of comb. "What about you?"

"My family died," Arul said.

"I'm so sorry," I told him.

"Don't worry. Christians go to heaven when they die."

"What do Christians do when they're alive?" I said, sensing he didn't want to dwell on the subject of his family's death. I had a vague idea that being Christian had something to do with worshipping Yesu, a God who wore a crown of thorns.

Arul started explaining all about Yesu, and about doing what a book called the Bible says to do.

Muthu joined us when Arul was telling me that Yesu said that if someone whacks you on one cheek, you should show them the other cheek.

"And if you do the things Yesu says to do," Muthu added,

"you sprout wings when you get to heaven so you can zoom about like an airplane—"

"You're Christian, too?" I asked Muthu.

"I don't know." Muthu scratched his chin.

"You are!" Arul said. "You repeated those words I told you to, remember?"

"Yes, yes," Muthu said. "But those are just words, and you told me to say them, boss, so I said them. But there's lots I don't really understand."

"Like what?" Arul demanded.

"Like that showing the other cheek thing. And like why didn't Yesu fight the bad guys?" Muthu continued. "He had twelve in his gang—"

"Not a gang!" Arul said. "Followers."

"Gangs follow the boss," Muthu argued. "So gangs are followers."

"Yesu had apostles," Arul corrected him. "Teachers who spread his word. Stop talking nonsense, Muthu. You should know better."

"Okay, okay, boss. I'll just turn around and show my other side." Muthu whipped about and wiggled his bottom at us.

Arul looked at the sky and moaned about how he didn't want our souls to burn in hell until the end of eternity. If I hadn't been laughing so hard, I'd have asked Arul how eternity could have an end.

"We're running late." Muthu glanced at an imaginary wrist-watch. "Need to get to the office, boss."

"Want to come with us?" Arul asked as he gathered the sacks and sticks they'd been carrying the day we first met.

"Yes, thanks. We really need a job," I said. "Where do you work?"

"We're adventurers," Muthu said. "We climb mountains every day. Right, boss?"

"Right," Arul said. "Although some days we swim across rivers instead."

"What do I need to bring?" I said.

"Don't worry, we'll find you what you need," Arul said.

"Rukku will bring beads." You patted your bead bag.

"Good idea." He grinned at you.

"Good," you agreed.

Kutti trotted along as we followed Arul across the bridge to the side we hadn't explored yet.

It led to a crowded street where cars honked and bicycle bells trilled and motorbikes and auto rickshaws spewed trails of smoke. A van lurched by, with schoolchildren in uniform hanging out the windows.

"One day, we'll go to school again, Rukku," I said. "Just like those kids."

"School!" Muthu guffawed, like I'd been joking. "You actually like school?"

"Not exactly," I admitted, thinking of the kids who teased us and the teachers who ignored us. "Not all the time. But there was one teacher I loved, and she said . . ." I paused, thinking of all the wonderful things she'd said—about my imagination and how smart I was—and how she'd encouraged us both. I realized the biggest gift she'd given me wasn't the book—it was something else. "She believed in me and Rukku."

"Believed what?" Muthu said.

"She said if we work hard"—I tried adopting Parvathi Teacher's persuasive tone—"we can do anything when we grow up."

"I used to go to school, when I lived in my village." Arul sounded wistful. "I had a great teacher, too."

"Don't sound so sad, boss," Muthu said. "We can do anything we want now, even though we aren't going to school. In fact, we can do anything we feel like *because* we don't have any schoolteacher telling us what to do!"

We turned onto a street full of wooden stalls. At one stall, flies swarmed up from an open gutter onto the skinned carcasses of goats. You held your nose.

"Think that's a bad smell?" Muthu cackled. "Wait till you get where we're going."

I couldn't imagine what could be worse. I remembered reading an article about a man who cleaned sewers—on an oily bit of newspaper in which Appa had wrapped pakoras to surprise us with on one of his good days. Surely we weren't going to clean sewers?

Finally, we stopped in front of a shack that had a peeling sign hanging above the open door—VICTORY WASTE MART.

"Kutti should wait outside," Arul said.

"Sit." You and Kutti and Muthu sat on the steps while I ducked into the shack after Arul.

Towers of junk—paper, plastic, glass, and metal—were stacked everywhere. A man was holding up a pair of rusty scales, weighing some cardboard.

"One sack, please, sir?" Arul asked.

The man's eyes fell on me. They were mean, like a rogue elephant's.

"What's your name, pretty girl?" the man asked.

I pretended I hadn't heard, figuring the less he knew about us, the better.

"Won't tell me your name, but you want my help?"

"Viji," I mumbled.

"New to the city? Where do you live?"

"Not sure," I said.

He motioned toward a pile of crumpled jute sacks lying in a corner. I took one, and Arul picked out a stick.

"Thank you, sir," Arul called over his shoulder.

We stepped out of the cluttered shack into the dazzling sunshine.

Arul shot me a concerned look. "You probably want to wait outside with Rukku and Kutti from now on?"

"Yes," I said, grateful he'd understood that the waste man scared me.

We cut through an empty park and past some teetering apartment buildings that at least offered us shade from the blazing sun. Huge posters as tall as we were, advertising the latest movies, were plastered on the walls. We followed Arul to a flat, open field, where there was no escape from the sunshine.

"Chee!" You wrinkled your nose.

Not far away was the largest garbage heap I'd ever seen. Mounds and mounds of junk and waste stretched out like a mountain range. The fragrance of wilted jasmine flowers mingled with the smell of goat droppings and every other bad smell imaginable.

"Welcome to the Himalayas of rubbish!" Muthu said with a dramatic flourish.

14

CLIMBING THE HIMALAYAS

You marched a few feet away from us, and away from the dump, and stood with your hands on your hips. Kutti stayed by your side.

"Sorry, Rukku," I said. "We have to stay."

"No, Viji," you said in a reasonable tone. "Go."

"We don't have a choice. Believe me, I don't love it here."

You pinched your nostrils shut.

"It's not the nicest place, but—it's—it's so we can stay together, Rukku."

You cocked your head.

"If I don't work here and earn money, we'll have to run right back to Appa. Understand?"

"Appa hit Viji," you said slowly. "Appa hit Amma."

My throat felt tight. You hadn't said anything about how he'd hit you.

"Viji and Rukku. Together." You came over and patted my cheek. "Rukku will make necklaces," you announced.

I hugged you tight.

"Where's Rukku going to sit?" Muthu said.

My eyes darted from one mound to another, wondering what to do, but you solved the problem yourself.

You found a plastic bucket to sit on under the shade of a thorny acacia tree, about as far from the rubbish range as you could go while staying within sight. You weren't as sheltered from the sun as I'd have liked, but there was nothing we could do about that.

You opened your bag and pulled out a long piece of string and knotted the end with a bead, so the rest wouldn't fall off. You worked quietly, your fingers sifting through the beads, searching for another that matched.

I had to start working, too.

"What do I do?" I hitched up my skirt as high as I could.

"Search." Muthu prodded a broken bottle at the base of a mound. "For treasure. Like this. Glass or metal scraps are best. The waste mart man will even buy cardboard and cloth if they're not too tattered."

Hesitantly, I prodded the mound closest to me. Nestling between a rusty can and a broken bottle was the carcass of a rat.

Nausea rippled through me, but I couldn't give up before I started. I tried to pick up the bottle with my stick, but it slid deeper into the rubbish.

"The waste mart man pays nicely for glass and metal, so we can't let it go." Arul grabbed the bottle with his bare hands and dropped it into my sack. "But this"—he jabbed at an empty juice carton and sent it tumbling farther down into the rubbish—"is worthless."

"Thanks. Sorry."

"Don't worry, you'll be an expert in no time."

I didn't say, *I don't want to become an expert ragpicker. I want to be a teacher.* With an effort, I swallowed my words and the bile that had risen in my throat and stepped farther into the mound.

The rubbish heap seemed to come alive as I walked through it, sucking at my slippers like a hungry beast. My feet sank into the slimy mess, and I lost sight of my toes. Flies swarmed around my ankles.

"Shuffle along, slowly, like you're wading through a river," Arul advised.

He made it sound easy, but it wasn't. I squelched along as best I could, making slow progress. I speared a damp rag and shook it into my sack. But when I spotted a bottle, half filled with sour milk, I had to reach for it with my bare hands.

I wanted to run away screaming. The only thing that kept me going was how peaceful you looked when I glanced back at you, sitting cross-legged, making another bead necklace, with Kutti, alert and attentive, next to you.

Arul must have realized what a slog it was for me, because every now and then, he called out, "Nice work."

We worked for so long with the sun beating down on our skin that my head started to hammer with pain, and it was a mercy when Arul finally said, "Enough. Let's stop."

My spirits sank even deeper when I compared their loot with mine. "I'm useless. I haven't got half as much as either of you."

"Don't worry." Arul peered into my sack. "Lots of good stuff in there. We have more, but it's not worth as much. You'll see."

Other than you, no one had ever shown me such loyalty.

Even half empty, my sack was heavier than anything I'd carried before. But with you humming softly as you put away your beads and our two new friends beaming at me like my sack was filled with precious gems, I shouldered my burden without complaint, my back straight, my steps light.

---◆---

15

EARNING OUR WAY

On the way to the waste mart, we stopped by a park where there was a small pond. I cupped my hands, gulped down some water, and then refilled our plastic bottle. Amma would never have let us drink water that wasn't boiled—but we didn't have a choice.

I stretched my aching arms and rinsed off my slippers. They were unrecognizably dirty, and so was my skirt, even though I'd hiked it up when I worked.

You and Kutti watched as the boys carefully separated our rubbish into piles: cardboard, metal, plastic, glass.

"Rukku wants to help," you told them.

"No," I said. "You could cut your hand on a rusty tin."

"Rukku wants to help!" you insisted. "Rukku wants to help!"

"If you don't mind," Arul said, "why don't we let her help?"

"You're joking," I said, though he sounded serious.

"Don't you ever let her do what she wants?" he said.

You stalked over to Arul.

"Viji, you've got to stop bossing her—"

"How dare you call me bossy!"

Arul softened his tone but not his words. "You're acting like you own Rukku. Muthu calls me boss, but I don't boss him around all the time."

His words pierced me like needles.

"Viji, I'm sorry. I see you're trying to protect your sister, but I bet she can do more than you think."

"Okay," I finally said. "Let Rukku help. But if she slices her hand in half—"

"You get to slice my hand in half?" Arul grinned.

"I get to slice your hands into little tiny pieces."

"Agreed."

So Arul showed you how to separate and sort the trash. As I watched you stacking pieces of cardboard and humming joyfully, the realization stabbed me that even I expected too little of you.

When you were done, your eyes shone. "Good work," you said to yourself.

He clapped you on the back. "That's right. You're the best helper."

"Best." You glanced at me, fierce with pride.

Even though I liked seeing you feel happy and valued, my stomach gave a tiny lurch as you and Arul smiled at each other. Until now, it had been just the two of us.

I jabbed the earth with my stick, ashamed at the twinge of jealousy. Arul deserved your affection, too. After all, he'd seen something in you that I hadn't bothered to notice. What else had I, who'd known and loved you so long, missed, that he'd discovered after knowing you less than a week?

"That's too much," I said, when Arul handed me half of what we'd earned that day. "I only collected about a quarter of what you two did."

"If I was too ill to collect anything tomorrow, what would you do?" Arul said.

"I'd share everything we had," I said.

"So, whatever money we earn belongs to all of us, equally, right?" Arul said. "That's how it's been with me and Muthu, and that's how we like it."

"Right, boss," Muthu said. "You want to stick with us, you play by our rules."

I felt too trembly to say thanks. A good kind of trembly. Not weak and fearful, like when we were home.

The rupee notes we'd earned were crumpled and dirty. One of them was torn off at the corner. Another had a brown smudge running across Mahatma Gandhi's face. But they looked beautiful to me.

Disgusting though the work had been, we finally had money all our own. Our money. I rubbed the notes between my fingers, as though they were fine silk. If we'd been rich, I'd have held on to them forever, just so I'd remember the feeling of freedom they'd given me.

We haggled with a handcart vendor for two big bunches of bananas, one ready to eat, the other still green, so it would ripen in a day or two. Then we stopped by a shack where brightly colored sweets were packed tight in glass jars, and you chose your favorite color—green.

"What would you two like for dinner?" Arul asked. "Your first earnings, so you get to choose."

"Rukku's probably happy with just fruit and sweets," I said, "but I'd like some biryani."

As we approached a street vendor whose spicy food was making my mouth water, a passerby in a faded sari wrinkled her nose and pulled her sari across her face.

With a shock, I realized that by climbing the Himalayas, we'd probably sunk lower in everyone's eyes than we'd been before.

"As much biryani as we can have," I said, handing over our cash to the vendor. My hand trembled. Did we look too scruffy to be served?

Luckily, the vendor was kind and even tossed a dry roti to Kutti. But as I gratefully took the warm package of food from him, he did ask us to get going. "Please don't hang around here. You'll drive away customers!"

You and the boys hurried back to the park with Kutti, but my feet dragged. Could we ever recover enough to clean ourselves up and go to school? Or was that dream as impossible as pretending the trash dump was a treasure trove?

"What are you waiting for, Akka? The food's going cold!" Muthu said as he settled down on a bench to eat. "Arul's done praying."

I slowly rolled the spicy yellow mixture of rice and vegetables and meat into little balls with my fingers and licked the sauce off my hands. You happily sucked on your sweet. Kutti scarfed up a bit of food that fell through Muthu's fingers.

Dusk was falling by the time we returned to our bridge, and I was glad. The darkness hid the dirt stains on my clothes from view.

—————————◆—————————

16

THE BLUE HILLS

The next morning, you took off down the far side of the bridge as we prepared for work.

"No, Rukku," I said. "We have to go to the Himalayas, and they're this way."

You crossed your arms over your chest and stood where you were.

"Actually, we don't *have* to do anything," Arul said. "The best part of this life is we can go wherever we want. We can go that way today, Rukku."

You beamed at him.

"In fact, it's best not to climb the Himalayas every day," Arul said. "Even though they're huge, we need to wait until people add some new old stuff."

"Plus, explorers can't go to the same place all the time," Muthu added. "It would get boring."

We walked beyond the wide, tree-lined avenues of the rich neighborhoods near the temple and the house where the gardener threw the orange at us, past smaller houses and shops where loudspeakers blared hit songs, and reached the poorest section of the city I'd yet seen. Shanties built out of every imaginable scrap of waste—roofs of coconut thatch or gunnysacks, walls cobbled together from metal signs, wooden crates, or even cardboard taped over with plastic sheets—lined the narrow streets.

"Look!" Arul cried. "The beach!"

Sure enough, in the distance beyond the shanties, past a long mound of rubbish, we could glimpse the sparkling blue ocean.

"We call this dump the Nilgiris," Muthu said. "The blue hills."

"Nicer than the Himalayas," I said. The reflection of the ocean and the sky gave the rubbish a bluish-gray tint, and the cool sea breeze made me like it better than the Himalayas, although I was sure the trash here was just as nasty.

"Pretty." You stared at the waves before settling down on a wooden crate and starting your beadwork. Kutti lay at your feet and shut his eyes.

A group of boys were already at work on the mound. Muthu and Arul ignored them and picked spots and got busy, but as soon as I reached for a bottle, one of the boys approached me.

"What do you think you're doing here?" He looked about as young as Muthu, but his clothes were even more ragged.

"What does it look like I'm doing?" I said. "Enjoying the view?"

"You have to give me a third of whatever you collect here," he said.

"Who made you the tax collector?" I said.

He spat right at me.

"Stop that!" Muthu popped up between us. "Leave my sister alone!"

"Who are you to tell me what to do?" The boy scowled at Muthu and waved his stick in my face.

"Stop it, Sridar!" An older boy, with fuzz on his upper lip, came up behind the one who threatened me. "I won't let you stay with us if you start fights."

Sullen faced, the boy named Sridar stepped away as Arul joined us.

"How are you, Kumar?" Arul said to the fuzzy-lipped boy.

"Look, this *is* our place," Kumar replied. "It's okay for you to come here, but you can't bring along every new kid in the city."

"Enough here for us all to share," Arul said.

"Yes, just look at this wealth spreading from sea to shore!" Muthu waved his stick. "Gray gold, I call it."

"We never acted like we owned the Himalayas," Arul said. "And I showed you where it was."

Kumar scowled but didn't argue anymore, and we all went back to work. After what felt like hours, my legs were coated with yellow and brown slime and my back was slick with sweat. A sense of hopelessness spread in my heart like the stains spreading on my skirt. Stains that would never wash out.

When I looked over at you, you were asleep. Your head was

slumped onto Kutti. I was worried you hadn't had enough to drink.

"We need to take a break," I said.

"Kumar's gang is still working," Muthu said.

"Life isn't a competition." Arul followed my gaze. "We have enough. Let's go."

I was so glad to leave that I didn't bother trying to retrieve my slippers, one of which had been sucked away, the other torn off as I squelched out of the rubbish to where you sat.

After all, the boys walked barefoot, and it didn't bother them.

17

HOW YOU BECAME A BUSINESSWOMAN

"I'll go to the waste man and meet you back at the bridge," Arul said. "You two should go and see the nice part of the beach with Muthu."

"Don't you want me to come and keep an eye on the scales to make sure the waste man doesn't cheat us?" Muthu said.

"I'll be fine," Arul insisted. "The girls are new to the city, and they deserve to see something nice after all the hard work."

So Muthu led us to what he called the "rich" section of the beach, where we could see sand dunes instead of trash hills, and my lungs filled with the welcome scents of salt and spray.

We strolled along the walkway between the road and the beach, past pushcarts piled high with corn and peanuts and hawkers selling multicolored plastic balls and cricket bats, flimsy kites, toys, dolls, pinwheels.

"Balloon?" you said hopefully. "Green balloon?"

"Not enough money," I said.

"Money?" You furrowed your brows thoughtfully. "Money?"

"You take a balloon from someone, you have to give them money," Muthu tried to explain, as I'd tried so many times before. "When we take bananas, we give the vendor our money. People sell their things for money."

"Sell necklaces?" you said. "Money?"

"Yes!" I was thrilled you'd understood. "That's how money works!"

"Sell necklaces." You sounded very pleased with yourself. "Get money. Get balloon."

"What a good idea!" Muthu patted you on the back. "We could sell your necklaces."

"Would anyone buy them?" I asked.

Muthu gestured at a vendor who was dozing in the shade of a pushcart piled high with the ugliest plastic dolls I'd ever seen. "If he's trying to sell those, why can't we try to sell her jewelry?"

So the two of you picked a spot on the walkway and arranged the six necklaces that you'd finished in a neat line.

"Necklaces for sale," Muthu sang out. "Pretty bead necklaces."

Groups of pedestrians bustled past without casting a glance in our direction. I was thinking we should give up when two girls walked by. They carried bags filled with books and looked old enough and well-dressed enough to be in college.

"How much?" one of the girls pointed to a necklace with red beads in which you'd tied your special loops and knots.

"Two hundred rupees," Muthu said.

I nearly fainted.

"One," the girl said.

"Two." Muthu held firm.

"Three," you said.

"Did you just raise the price instead of lowering it?" She smiled at you. "Three?"

"Four," you said.

"My sister means one hundred fifty rupees," I said.

"Three," you sang. "Three, four, five, six."

"I'd better pay before the price soars ever higher." The girl laughed and then fished in her bag for her money.

"I can't believe you're actually spending your money on that," the other girl exclaimed.

"What's a hundred and fifty rupees?" the nice girl said. "These kids are cute, and the necklaces are pretty."

"Pretty." You wrapped one around a finger and twirled it so the beads caught the sunlight.

"That's right." The girl slid her necklace over her head. "Very pretty."

We couldn't have asked for a better model. The girl's golden brown skin set off the beads, making them sparkle even more.

"We'll send some friends your way," she promised.

Sure enough, another college girl came by soon, her pink sari swishing around her heels. "There you are! I'll take one."

"Which one?" I asked.

"Whichever, doesn't matter."

"One hundred and fifty." I handed over a pink one to match her sari.

She gave me two hundred.

I returned the extra fifty.

"Keep it," she said.

"We settled on one hundred and fifty," I said. "We don't need charity."

"You're not offended, are you?" She sounded worried. "I'm sorry."

"Not offended," I said.

In less than an hour, you'd sold all but one necklace and we had earned a small fortune.

"You're a miracle, Rukku!" I said. "Your necklaces are worth their weight in gold!"

"Golden roasted corn," Muthu said dreamily. "Rukku is a miracle, Kutti, do you know that?"

Kutti opened his mouth wider, like he was grinning in agreement.

"Balloon!" you said.

We walked with you to the balloon stand, though I worried about whether buying a balloon was really such a good idea. Amma had bought us a huge balloon once, and we had fun with it until it burst and the loud noise set you off.

But my worry dwindled when I looked at you.

Standing erect, an openmouthed smile spread wide across your face, you picked out a long, bottle-green balloon.

"You give him the money, Rukku. You earned it." I counted out the exact amount and put it into your outstretched palm.

You handed over the money. I'd never seen you stand so tall before.

That was something.

No.

That was everything.

"Where did you get all this . . ." Arul's eyes darted from your balloon to our clothes to the food we'd piled on the ground in front of our tents—a whole loaf of fresh white bread, chocolate bars, packages of salty plantain chips and crisp murukkus.

We'd felt so rich, we'd even bought Kutti a juicy bone from the mutton stall, and he was gnawing on it contentedly.

You handed Arul the new T-shirt we'd bought him, and then tied your balloon to our tent.

"Look!" Muthu unfurled our straw mats. "These are for us to sleep on!"

"What? How?" Arul leaned against the bridge wall like he was too surprised to stand.

"It's all because of Rukku!" I said.

Bit by bit, we told him how you'd sold your necklaces.

"That's wonderful," Arul said. "Thank you, Rukku."

"Thank you, Rukku. Thank you, Rukku," Muthu chanted.

"Thank you, Rukku," you repeated, swatting at your balloon. "Thank you, Rukku."

You and Muthu played with your balloon while Arul and I placed the straw mats and new pillows inside the tents, making them look almost cozy.

"Fly, balloon?" You pulled it close to your ear as if you could hear it reply, the way I'd seen you talk to your wooden doll. "Okay," you decided, untying the balloon. "Go."

"No!" Muthu made a grab for it, but it floated out of reach.

I was just as surprised as he sounded, but my surprise was mixed with happiness and relief. Ever since we'd left, you'd been behaving so differently from before. You hadn't once lost your temper. You'd made friends. You even looked different, because you'd been holding your back straight all the time.

"Why did you let it go, Rukku?" Muthu said grumpily.

"Balloon wants to fly." You waved as it drifted above the river.

"But—" Muthu began.

"You set it free, Rukku," I cut him short. "Now it can go anywhere it feels like. That was really nice of you."

When we were done eating, I showed Arul the remaining notes and coins that I'd refused to let us spend. "We've still got some money left."

"We could go to a movie tonight," Muthu suggested.

"No," I said. "We're going to save it."

"I saw a movie one time with Rajinikanth acting." Muthu boxed an imaginary opponent. "I can still hear Rajinikanth punching the bad guy. Tishoom."

"Tishoom." You looked up briefly, then continued playing with Kutti. "Tishoom."

"See? Rukku thinks it's a good idea."

"She didn't say that at all. Arul, don't *you* think we should save some money?"

"Where?" Arul sounded genuinely curious. "How?"

"Think they'll let us enter a bank?" Muthu chuckled.

"Why not?" I said.

"Now that we're wearing T-shirts without holes, I'm sure they won't mind." Muthu fingered a hole in his shorts. "Especially if we spray on our perfume and wash our feet."

I glanced down at my skirt. I'd tried so hard to scrub off the stains that I'd torn a hole right through it. Beneath the hem, my toenails peeped out, edged with dirt.

I tried calculating how much money we could make if we switched to the bead business. "Rukku finishes two or three necklaces a day. Let's say we sell each one for just fifty rupees each, and we only manage to sell about ten every week. Even then we'll make around—"

"Ai! Stop it, Akka," Muthu said. "All this planning ahead is making my head hurt."

"Don't you ever think about the future?" I challenged him.

"No," Muthu said. "There's enough to worry about every day without worrying about tomorrow."

"I don't just *worry* about tomorrow," I said. "I also imagine good things. But all sorts of bad stuff could happen, so we should plan in case—"

"That's right," Muthu interrupted. "All sorts of bad things *can* happen, and that's why we should spend the money, Akka."

"You should imagine good things, too." I couldn't—wouldn't—let the boys destroy my hope we'd find a better life, somehow. "I don't know how you live without dreams."

"The only way I can get through each day," Arul said quietly, "is by not thinking of all those tomorrows. All those minutes and days and months and years of sorting through mountains of rubbish. But if it helps you to have a bit of money to hold on to, we'll save some for you to dream on."

Muthu grumbled as I stashed our remaining notes and coins in a pothole on the bridge and covered them with stones, promising myself I'd find some way to make the boys see how important our dreams were.

One day, you'd have a bead shop, I'd be a teacher, and the boys would do work they liked. Because our treasure trove was sure to grow, thanks to you.

19

ABOVE A SILVER RIVER

I was savoring the sound of Muthu's snores rising and falling in concert with yours, after telling you our bedtime tale, when I heard Arul sneaking out of his tent.

I felt too excited to sleep, so I sneaked out to join him.

Arul was sitting by a break in the bridge wall, watching the river. "Looks like silver, doesn't it? You could make up a story about a silver river."

"You could make up stories, too, you know." I sat next to him.

"I'm no good at telling stories. My brother was. But not as good as you."

"What sort of stories did he tell?"

"Stories about Yesu. From the Bible. Once, Yesu had just five loaves of bread and two fishes, and he turned it into enough food to feed a whole crowd."

"Too bad Yesu isn't here now," I said. "That's a useful trick."

"It was a miracle, not a trick." Arul's eyes shone, bright as the moonlit river. "If you'd heard my brother tell that story, you'd believe it. Or if you heard my priest tell it. Our priest was the best. He ran our village school. He taught us everything— math and reading and writing—as well as songs and prayers."

"Sounds like my favorite teacher," I said.

"My whole family loved him. We all loved music, too. My brother and sister and mother sang really well. My dad just sang really loud, loud and happy, though always out of tune." Arul laughed. "But my dad was the best fisherman in our village. He'd bring home ten times as much as the other fishermen. He used to call the ocean Kadalamma. Ocean Mother."

"That's a nice name," I said.

"Yes. Too nice. What actually happened was that the 'ocean mother' took my real mother away. And my sister and my brother and my father. One day, the sea receded so far that fish were hopping on the ground. Everyone else ran in, laughing, to gather up the fish. Only I hung back. I was scared, seeing the ocean act so strangely. And then it rose and came at us like a monstrous cobra, swallowing everything in sight, and I ran."

I could hardly take in what he was telling me, about how everyone he'd loved had disappeared in one terrible moment.

"Don't know why I ran," Arul whispered. "Wouldn't have if I'd known they'd all be taken. But, soon enough, I'll meet them again in heaven."

He spoke with complete conviction. And I realized that by

holding on to his beliefs, he was holding on to his family. He was so sure he'd be reunited with them when he died that he didn't care how long he lived.

But I cared. I cared about him as strongly as if we'd known each other all our lives. I couldn't imagine our future without him and Muthu in it. I searched for the right words to tell him so, but all I finally said was "I hope it'll be years and years before you get to go to your heaven."

"Yes. I guess I'll have to wait a long time." He sighed. "I've always wondered why God left me behind." Then he gave me a crinkly smile. "Maybe he knew I needed to make friends with the three of you."

"Four of us, not three," I corrected. "Don't forget Kutti. He's part of our family, too."

"Four," he agreed. "I was never good at mathematics."

20

♦

ENDLESS MOUNTAINS

"Couldn't we all learn to make necklaces?" I suggested the next morning. "We'd get so much more money."

"But if we stop providing the waste man with stuff every day, he might start paying us less," Muthu argued. "Plus, Kumar's gang could take over."

"The city'll have trash every day, but those girls aren't going to buy necklaces every day," Arul added. "Who knows if we'll find other customers?"

"Also," Muthu said, "most people won't pay as much as those college girls."

"How many necklaces do we even have left, Rukku?" Arul asked.

"One." You fished out the necklace we hadn't yet sold and let it dangle from your fingers. Kutti pounced on a beam of light the necklace caught and reflected onto the bridge. "One. One. One-two-three."

"Just one? So, we don't even have enough to make a nice display," Muthu said. "Let's go back to the Himalayas. Rukku can do her work while we do ours."

I agreed because I didn't want to offend them by pushing too hard for what I felt was a nicer way to earn a living. After all, there'd be time to figure this out. I could, slowly but surely, convince them. I shouldered my bag and picked up my stick and tried to put on a brave face.

"Ready to climb the Himalayas again?" Muthu asked when we arrived at the dump.

My disgust probably showed, because Arul took one quick look at me and tried to make it into a game. "You can be captain," he said.

"What?"

"We're mountain climbers, remember? You can lead our team." Arul speared a large rag with a misshapen metal pole that lay on the ground. "Here—carry our flag, Captain."

"Okay." I took the flag from Arul and stood straight as a soldier, singing the national anthem. "Jana, gana, mana . . ."

You set your beads down and hummed the tune along with me, and Kutti stuck his nose in the air and yowled.

I was just getting into the spirit of our game when someone

hooted, "Look, Kumar! Those bridge boys are following that new girl!"

It was Sridar, the rude boy who'd wanted to fight. Scowling, I faced him.

"Aha! So she's your leader now?" another one of Sridar's gang mocked me.

"Why not?" Arul asked.

"But . . ." Sridar gaped. "She's a girl!"

"Indira Gandhi was a woman," Arul said. "She led our country, didn't she?"

"These boys don't know that, boss," Muthu said. "They're ignorant."

"Who are you insulting?" Sridar balled his fists.

"You started it." Muthu glared back, arms akimbo.

"Never mind who started it." Arul pushed them apart. "I'm stopping it. We need to get to work. All of us."

"Right," Kumar agreed.

"Let's see who gets more stuff," Sridar challenged as he moved off with the three other boys in his gang. "That'll show who's smarter."

"Tell us where to start, Captain," Arul said.

I marched toward a mound that looked like it had lots of glass and tin. Carefully, I waded up as high as I could. I stuck our flag at the top and saluted it. The boys saluted me, and we went to work.

A nauseating smell rose and smacked me in the face, but I

toiled as fast as I could. I tried to focus on the one thing I could be thankful for—the thick haze of rain clouds that kept the sun from beating down on you and the rest of us.

Finally, our sacks were full. "Enough," I commanded.

We marched back, single file, with me in the lead, to where you were waiting patiently.

"Finish up," Sridar yelled to his gang as we left.

We hurried along to the waste mart man's street. We were busy sorting our loot out front when Sridar sneaked up and snatched a twisted metal plate that we'd found.

"Give it back!" Muthu shouted. "It's ours!"

"Not anymore." Sridar shoved Muthu backward.

"Muthu?" You leaped up as he lost his balance and fell. "Owwa?"

Kutti snarled and nipped Sridar's ankle, making him yelp.

"I'm okay, Rukku." Muthu grinned. "But sounds like Sridar has an owwa."

Arul was pulling Kutti off when Kumar and the other boys in his gang joined Sridar, yelling and adding to the commotion.

The waste mart man lumbered out of his shack and took in the scene. "What's going on?"

I grabbed your hand and looked down at my grime-encrusted feet.

"Who's this?" He towered over us, so close that his shadow fell across you. "Another new girl?"

"Hairy nose," you observed, looking up at him. "Hairy ears."

A nervous giggle escaped me. Some of the boys giggled, too.

"Think that's funny?" He looked at you. "What's your name?"

"Rukku," you answered.

"Rrruuukkku," he exaggerated the slowness of your speech. "Where do you live?"

"Don't answer him, Rukku," I whispered.

"Keeping secrets?" The waste mart man turned to Kumar's gang. "Maybe one of *you* boys can tell me where these girls stay."

"They live on the bridge," Sridar volunteered.

"Shut up!" Kumar hissed. "Sneaks can't stay with us." He stepped away from Sridar, and the other boys in his gang followed.

"*On* a bridge?" The waste mart man scratched his nose. "Which bridge?"

Kumar pressed his lips together.

"I don't like doing business with rude kids who don't reply to me," the waste man growled. "Rude kids get paid less."

No one, not even Sridar, said another word.

"How could anyone live *on* a bridge without getting run over by traffic?" the waste man said, but he didn't press us with any more questions. He even paid us the same pittance he usually did, despite his threats.

Still, the waste man's curiosity left me uneasy.

21

◆

CHASED AWAY

We spent some of our skimpy earnings on thick plastic sheets to keep our home dry, because Arul said the rainy season was approaching.

"It scares me that the waste man's so interested in where we live," I told Arul that evening as we spread plastic on the ground beneath our straw mats and pillows. "You don't think he'll come looking for us, do you?"

"No." Arul sounded confident. "He's a cheat and a bully, but too lazy to come searching for us."

"What are you worrying about now, Akka?" Muthu cackled with laughter. "Scared he's going to steal our gold?"

"You two don't think we should move?" I said.

"What, and give up our palace above the silver river?" Arul said.

"Don't worry, he's scared of me." Muthu flexed his scrawny arms. "See how much muscle I have?"

And with you and Kutti and the boys close at hand—and the waste mart man far away—it felt silly to worry.

———————

Later that night, I was falling asleep to the patter of light rain when a volley of barks interrupted the peace. I peered out of our tent.

Kutti was standing by the entrance with his back arched.

"What's wrong?" came Arul's sleepy voice.

A man cursed, and another man yelled something back. I recognized one of the voices. The waste mart man had found us.

Arul lifted the towel separating our tents. "Quick," he said. "Run."

"Rukku." I shook you awake. "Get up!"

Muthu and I each took one of your hands and pulled you out of the tent. We began to hobble across the rain-slicked bridge.

"Rrruuukkku," I heard the waste mart man drawl as he and the other man stumbled toward us, "I've found you."

"Our money!" Muthu gasped. "I've got to go back for it."

"We can get it later!" Arul shoved Muthu forward. "Keep going!"

We stumbled on, but Arul stopped to fling a chunk of concrete at the men. Snarling, Kutti hurled himself in their direction. I heard a yowl of pain. Kutti or one of the men?

When we reached the road, Kutti and Arul raced up to join us.

"You two hide," Arul whispered. "We'll lead them away."

In the dim glow of a streetlamp, I saw Muthu's and Arul's bare heels thumping along the dark road ahead. Then the boys slowed down, running in full view, hoping to lure the men after them.

The two of us turned in to a side street, and we stiffened against a wall in the shadows. I tried not to think of anything except the feel of your hand, bony but strong, in mine.

We were lucky. The men hurtled down the other road, after the boys.

You slouched over Kutti and mewed like a lost kitten. An occasional car whooshed by.

At last, Arul and Muthu arrived, panting.

"Come on," Arul said. "We've got to find a better hiding place."

You wouldn't budge, though the boys whispered encouragements.

"Rukku," I urged. "Please. We have to go just a little bit farther."

Slowly, you straightened up, like a snail coming out of its shell, and let us haul you along.

We sped down a quiet stretch of road where huge trees loomed over us.

"Here." Arul stopped by a long wall. "Come on."

Arul climbed atop the wall and leaned down.

"Rukku first." I struggled to lift you as high as I could, and Arul pulled you over the wall. I heard you land with a faint thump.

Kutti's sharp eyes had discovered a hole, and he was scuffling through it.

Muthu clambered over the wall with Arul's help, and then it was my turn.

The wet wall gleamed in the faint moonlight. I slipped a few times but finally scaled it and plummeted into bushy under-growth on the other side.

It was when Arul thudded down next to me that I noticed we were in a graveyard.

22

◆

THE GRAVEYARD

I looked around the graveyard but couldn't find you. "Where's Rukku?"

"She couldn't have gone far." Arul glanced nervously into the shadows. "Kutti's disappeared, too—he must be with her."

"We have to find them." My voice came out all panicky. I had a vision of a ghost swallowing you whole. "Let's split up and search."

Something rustled the branches of a tree.

"I am not scared," Muthu announced in a thin voice. "I am not scared . . ."

We walked a few feet farther into the graveyard, and suddenly you popped out right in front of us, from where you must have curled up—on top of a grave.

Muthu squealed.

"Quiet, you fool," Arul said. "It's just Rukku!"

"I know," Muthu claimed, though his voice was all shaky. "I was just pretending to be scared. For fun."

You curled up in a tight ball again, and I threw my arms around you.

Kutti sat nearby, his ears pricked up.

"You should be scared of those living men on the bridge, Muthu," Arul said "Not scared of these dead ones."

He was right. The living posed a greater threat. Yet my skin still felt clammy, and my throat dry.

"Can't believe you wanted to run back just to get our money," Arul scolded Muthu. "You might have ended up in a graveyard."

"I did end up in a graveyard," Muthu retorted.

"Dead in a graveyard," Arul said.

"Those men couldn't squish an ant dead," Muthu said. "They were too muddled to aim their blows properly."

You whimpered, and I stroked your back. For days, you'd been so much surer of yourself. Now your fists were clenched tight, like they used to be when Appa was angry.

You were silent for what felt like forever. Then you whispered, "Go back? Bridge?"

"We have to stay here now. We had to run away from those men, like we ran away from Appa."

"Amma," you whispered.

"I miss her, too. But we're together."

Squeezing my hand tight, you buried your face in Kutti's fur.

"It's good we moved," Arul said. "See what flat beds we have here, Rukku? Nice and cool."

"Beds?" You patted your grave, tentatively, like you were considering his words. "Nice? Cool?"

"That's right." I forced myself to sound as bright as possible.

"High-class hotel we're staying in," Muthu piped up. "But despite the super beds, I'll climb that big banyan tree over there and sleep somewhere up in the branches."

"Oh, up where the ghosts live?" Arul said. "I've heard ghosts usually hide in banyan tree branches."

"Or right here on the grass." Muthu stretched himself out.

"The grass is wet," I said. "You'll catch cold."

"Pick out your very own grave, Muthu." Arul spread his hands expansively. "So many to choose from."

The drizzle had stopped, and the moon was peeping out from behind the clouds.

"Come, Rukku," Arul continued, "let's show Muthu what to do." He took you by the hand and led you around, making a big show of touching each grave, like he was testing them for smoothness.

Muthu stopped at the grave closest to the one Arul chose.

Arul peered through the darkness until he could make out the inscription on the grave marker. "So, Muthu is going to sleep above Mr. Vincent's remains. Thank you, Mr. Vincent. Now, your turn, Rukku. Which one do you want?"

You chose another one close by and lay back. I sat beside you and smoothed your brow.

You shivered for a long time, whether from fear or being wet by the cool drizzle, I wasn't sure. When you finally grew still, I thought you'd fallen asleep. But then you said, "Story?"

"Story," Muthu agreed.

"Story," Arul echoed.

"Once upon a time," I said, "two sisters and two brothers lived in a magical land."

"About time you added us," Muthu said. I could hear a smile in his voice.

23

WEDDING BREAKFAST

When I finally woke, I couldn't tell what the hour was, because the sky was overcast. The drone of bloodthirsty mosquitoes had woken me several times during the night, and my arms itched with bites. Trying not to scratch at them, I got up and stretched.

"Wake up, sleepyheads!" Arul called to me and Muthu.

You and Arul were already exploring the far corner of the graveyard, where the grass looked as unkempt as the boys' hair. Not that ours was in a much better state.

"What a good place to hide," I said. The inscriptions had worn off many of the grave markers, and most looked like they hadn't been tended in years. The high wall teetered in some places, but mostly it hid us from view of the road. "Lonelier and more neglected than our bridge."

"What are we going to do for breakfast?" Muthu yawned. "I'm hungry."

"Hungry," you agreed.

"You'll be delighted to hear," Arul announced, "we've been invited to a wedding breakfast."

"Wedding?" I said.

"Yes. I forgot all about that wedding, boss." Muthu winked at Arul, and then he wound an imaginary turban on his head. "Is my turban on straight?"

"Yes, but it's not as fancy as mine," Arul said.

"Dum, dum, dum." Muthu started marching, beating on an imaginary drum. "You want to join the wedding procession, Rukku?"

I didn't ask the boys what they were up to, because I was thrilled to see you return his smile, like your confidence and courage were resurging.

"Dum, dum, dum." You walked alongside Muthu. "Dum, dum, dum."

Arul followed, playing an imaginary pipe.

We'd lost our home, but you three were still cheerful, and I tried to forget my worries and be content with that.

———

"It's as large as my fairy-tale palace!" I gazed at the wedding hall from a nearby hill, where we'd stopped to rest. "Just the sight of it's worth that long walk!"

We could see over a low white wall and right into the pillared room where a newlywed couple sat cross-legged opposite the priests. The bride wore so many jewels, she looked like one of the trees strung with strands of twinkling lights in the surrounding garden.

"Rich people," Muthu said. "They've stuck lights on the trees even though it's daytime."

The music in the hall rose to a crescendo, the beat of drums and the whine of the nadhaswaram so loud, we could catch the sound.

"Why do they play that silly pipe when people get married?" Muthu said. "It sounds like a frog with a sore throat."

"Pretty." You hummed, slightly off-key. "Pretty."

"Right." Arul smiled at you. "Stay quiet, Muthu, you uncultured brat. Rukku and I are enjoying the concert."

The crowd of guests stood and showered the couple with rose petals. "Perfect timing," Arul said. "They'll move to the dining room next. It's around the back. Come on."

As guests lined up to congratulate the couple, we walked downhill and around the hall to the back, where the open windows allowed us a glimpse of long tables on which banana leaf plates had been laid out. Servers came in bearing huge pots of steaming food.

"Ah, what a spread!" Muthu sounded entranced.

I was more impressed by how much the guests didn't eat, as the servers cleared away banana leaves still piled high with food.

"Here comes *our* feast," Muthu said as a man came and stuffed some bags into the dumpster outside the back gate of the wedding hall.

When he was gone, Muthu skipped over to the dumpster and shooed away a couple of bedraggled crows that were hovering above it. He lifted out an untouched, unpeeled banana and waved it triumphantly in the air. Then another. And another.

He handed them all to you.

Arul joined him, and the boys discovered even more: golden laddu balls, some half eaten, some barely touched. I couldn't imagine throwing away a sweet—just wasting the whole thing. Actually I couldn't even imagine wasting one bite of such a mouthwatering delicacy.

Ignoring the dirt caking my fingernails, trying to forget that these were a stranger's leftovers, I stuck a sweet in my mouth.

"So good," Arul mumbled with his mouth full. "Try some, Rukku." We were all so hungry that Arul had forgotten about praying.

"Yech," you said.

"Laddus aren't your favorite? Want to try a different sweet?" Muthu picked off the bits of rice and vegetables that were stuck to a ball of syrupy gulab jamun and handed it to you. "You'll like this. Smells of rose petals."

"Sweet?" You sniffed suspiciously at the dark, sticky ball and then nibbled at it as daintily as a princess, while the rest of us hungrily cleaned off one leaf plate after another.

"Look, Rukku." Muthu motioned at the cloud of flies that hovered around us. "Our meals are so delicious that uninvited guests always visit."

A skinny cow ambled over. Kutti barked at it.

"Shhup!" you said to Kutti, placing a finger across your lips.

"As I was saying," Muthu said. "Uninvited guests—coming in all sizes!"

The cow edged away, but you rolled up one of the empty banana leaves and held it out to the cow.

It started chewing placidly. You leaned against the cow's side and crooned to it.

24

♦

BELIEVING AND IMAGINING

"That was some feast." Muthu wiped his mouth with the back of his hand. "Now I feel ready for anything."

"Good," Arul said. "We should go and see what's left—if anything—of our stuff."

"Captain Rukku"—Muthu saluted you—"let's march to the bridge and see what we can salvage."

You and Kutti led the way, and we arrived at our bridge to find it looking like a battlefield, with our belongings scattered everywhere.

A few brightly colored shreds of cloth fluttered gaily where our tent had been. Caught on a piece of iron that stuck out of the concrete wall, a ragged T-shirt hung, limp as a flag of surrender.

"Can't believe they ripped up everything they got their ugly hands on," I said.

"That T-shirt was ripped up anyway." Muthu shrugged. "No big loss there. And they didn't tear up everything. Look! Our tarps are here."

But you were not consoled. Tears welled in your eyes. "No! No! No!"

Kutti rubbed himself against your legs, and you crouched down and hugged him. I slumped by the bridge wall, right next to you.

"All gone." You stroked a frayed knot of the rope that had once held our roof together.

"That's not true." Muthu bent to pick up a tiny bead that glittered near his foot. "See this? Maybe we can find some more."

You took the bead from him, and your face brightened slowly, like the sun peeking out from behind rain clouds. The two of you started collecting what remained of your beads, while I searched for the hollow in which I'd hidden our money. And it was there!

"Here's the money we saved," I announced.

"And here's your book!" Arul brought it over to me and showed me how the previous night's drizzle had left some pages stuck together.

Damp though it was, I pressed it against my chest. It comforted me even more than the money. Parvathi Teacher's gift felt like a piece of my dream that I could hold on to, a sign that though we'd lost so much, we'd find a way to go on.

You came over to me, rolling a bead between your fingers, and we linked arms.

"We can make a nice new home." Muthu patted the tarps.

"Maybe right here? That old tent was flimsy, and now we've got a chance to make a better one."

"No," I said. "What if the men come back?"

"Yes. The graveyard is safer," Arul said. "No one will look for us there."

"But it'll never be home!" Muthu said.

"This wasn't either," Arul said.

"Of course it was!" Muthu said. "So what if it didn't have a fine roof or walls? It's the best place I ever lived in. Except for Rukku and Akka's palace."

"That palace is imaginary!" Arul said. "You've never lived there, none of us has."

"Our palace *is* a home, inside my head," Muthu insisted. "And those men can't wreck it. Ever."

"Yes," I said. "We will always have our palace." I went over to him and put an arm around his shoulders. "And I promise we'll fix up a home at the graveyard, too."

With my toes, I scuffed at the crumbling concrete wall of the bridge. I thought of the money we'd spent trying to make our tent cozy. Ruined though the bridge was, there was something magical about living above the shining river. Even on that bleak day, it felt more like home than the dingy apartment where we'd stayed with our parents.

"I hate leaving, too, Muthu," I said. "But we have no choice. And we have to find work soon. Our money won't last long. Rukku has hardly any beads left, and we can't risk returning to the Himalayas. It's too close to the waste mart man's place."

"We don't have to go to the Himalayas," Arul said. "Haven't you noticed there are junk heaps everywhere? Plenty of other places we can work. And other waste mart men."

"That's right, Akka. Don't worry." Muthu inhaled noisily. "This is one big sweet-smelling city. We know every neighborhood by the scent of its garbage. You'll be an expert, too, really soon."

"Wonderful," I muttered. "My life's aim was to map the city's dumps."

"We'll be all right," Arul said. "We can buy more beads, and you can try to make a go of Rukku's necklace business, like you'd wanted. After all, it's thanks to you and her that we've still got any money left."

"Yes!" I said, glad that Arul had finally agreed we needed to do more with your bead business.

"While the two of us work at the dump, you two can get more beads," Arul said. "But first, let's drop our stuff off at the graveyard."

As we walked away, you and Muthu started playing a game, tossing a bit of concrete into the air like a ball and trying to catch it again before it fell. Kutti was following along, his nose moving up and down. I watched, glad you were staying so strong, although our lives kept going up and down, like the broken concrete bit you were tossing and catching.

25

CANDLES IN THE DARK

Arul didn't lead us straight back to the graveyard. He took us down a street we hadn't seen before.

"There's a church right by here," Arul said. "Let's go there and buy a candle to give thanks to God."

"Thanks?" Muthu stared at him. "For what?"

I couldn't believe my ears either. "You're thanking God the waste man took away everything we had?"

"The waste man didn't take away everything we had," Arul said. He threaded my free hand through one of his and reached out for you with his other hand.

"See?" Arul said. And I saw.

We stood in a circle, linked together like an unbreakable necklace.

"No dogs allowed," Arul said when we arrived at the church. "Can you get him to stay here and wait for us, Rukku?"

"Wait." You patted his head. "Wait."

"We'll be right back, Kutti," I said. "Look after our stuff."

"Because surely our stuff is so precious, anyone who sees it would want to steal it," Muthu joked as we laid down the bundle of things we'd salvaged from the bridge.

As Arul shut the church door behind us, Kutti whined softly, but you didn't seem to hear him. You and I had only seen churches from the outside. Inside, the church was dark and quiet. Faint streams of light danced in through rainbow-colored windows. Straight ahead, instead of a stone image of a God or Goddess, hung a wooden cross with a carved figure of Yesu, bleeding, with thorns wound around his head.

"Owwa!" you whispered. "Owwa!"

"It's just a statue, Rukku," I whispered back. "It's not alive."

"It's God," Arul said in a reverent tone. Then he led us to a place where rows of candles were flickering. He dropped a coin into a box and lit a candle.

"We thank Yesu and Mary Amma," he explained, "by lighting candles. And we pray they'll keep us safe."

"Isn't it enough if we just pray?" I said. "Must we actually burn our money?"

Muthu chuckled.

Arul placed his candle beside the others. You watched as intently as when you made your bead necklaces.

Then he held a candle out to you.

"Careful, Rukku. That flame can give you an owwa," I said. Even though I knew how good you were with your hands, I couldn't help warning you. After all, you'd never held a burning candle before. Worrying about your safety was a habit I couldn't cure, and I hoped I didn't sound bossy. "Wax drips, and it's hot."

Arul placed his hands over yours, so you were holding the candle together. I watched you set it in place.

"Again?" you said.

Muthu and I flopped down on a smooth wooden bench and watched as Arul let you buy and light one more candle. And then another.

Your hand trembled slightly, but your gaze was steady with concentration, your tongue between your teeth.

"Enough?" I suggested, but you ignored me.

"She's hearing the voice of God," Arul whispered.

"Too bad she can't hear my voice, telling her to stop spending all our money on candles," I whispered to Muthu. "Soon we won't have any money left."

But you were so in awe that I decided not to argue.

You seemed to melt right into that moment, kneeling before the candles, your eyes fixed on the moving flames.

And they were so beautiful, those little flames, dancing in that still, silent church, dancing like they could hear music. Like they were alive. Alive the way you were alive, alive right there, right then, not worried about what might happen in a few hours or days, not remembering what had happened before.

I heard a sudden snap, the sound breaking my—but not your—reverie. A kind-looking woman who must have been watching us the whole time had snapped open her handbag and started riffling through it. Our eyes met.

"We're not beggars." I assumed she was looking to give us some change.

"It's not money." She held out a small rectangular card. "Can you read?"

"Of course." I snatched the card out of her hands and read it aloud, to prove I wasn't lying. "Dr. Celina Pinto. Director, Safe Home for Working Children." Below that was an address—a number and the name of a street that sounded familiar. A street I remembered in the nicer part of town.

"I'm Celina Aunty," she said. "I run a home for children and help place them in schools or learn a trade."

"School!" My excited shout echoed through the church. At last I'd found a person who could fulfill my dreams.

"We don't need free stuff," Arul grunted. "We work."

"Our children work," she said. "They pay for what I provide by working for me, keeping the place clean, obeying my rules. No smoking, no lying, no stealing."

"Stealing?" A man wearing a long robe entered through a door I hadn't seen, right by the altar. He glanced down at us anxiously. "These strays are trying to steal, Dr. Celina?"

"They're not stealing, Father. They're lighting candles," Celina Aunty started to explain.

But the boys didn't wait to hear any more.

"Come on, Akka." Muthu scampered out of the church. Arul pulled you out, and I followed. You blinked sulkily in the sunshine that had briefly broken through the clouds.

"Now you want to find another church, boss?" Muthu said to Arul. "So we can give thanks this priest didn't accuse us of stealing and send us to a policeman?"

"Priests don't accuse kids who are in God's house," Arul said, but he didn't sound very certain.

"Well, it's a good thing that priest showed up," I said, "or we'd have spent every last coin on candles."

"Did you see the faith on Rukku's face?" Arul said. "Her soul's going to heaven, for sure. With mine."

"Good for your souls," I said. "But can we please use what's left of our money to take care of our stomachs, too?"

26

PRETEND PRINCESSES

Silver pins of rain fell around us as we left the church. I cast an uneasy glance at the sky. The rainy season had started, and though it was only drizzling now, in the days ahead, we'd face many downpours. Some years, the monsoon was terrible, and it poured nonstop.

"Tea?" You scratched at a mosquito bite on your elbow. "Tea!"

"What a good idea, Rukku! Let's visit Teashop Aunty. Maybe she even has some beads left."

I told the boys about Teashop Aunty, and after agreeing to meet back at the graveyard, we parted ways. The boys went to find a new waste mart man, and you and I and Kutti walked toward the teashop.

We went around the back. I knocked hesitantly on the back door, and a smiling Teashop Aunty came to greet us.

"Viji! I wondered how you were getting on! And Rukku! You look so much taller, standing so straight and nice."

"Rukku looks nice," you agreed, holding your chin even higher than before.

"It's good to see you again, Aunty," I said.

"Stay there a moment, and I'll bring you a cup of tea." Although Aunty sounded genuinely pleased to see us again, she didn't invite us Into her kitchen. Not that I blamed her, given how scruffy we'd become.

In a few minutes Teashop Aunty returned with two Styrofoam cups filled with steaming, milky tea.

"Now, tell me, Viji," she said as we blew on our tea to cool it. "How are you doing?"

"My friends and I sell trash to make ends meet," I said. "But Rukku makes necklaces—like you taught her to—and sells them. Only, we've run out of beads. May we borrow some more, if you have some?"

"Of course." Teashop Aunty disappeared into her kitchen again, and emerged with a small package of beads—many fewer and not as pretty as the first set she'd given us, but enough to get you going again. "I kept these for you, Rukku, hoping you'd come back."

"Beads!" You pressed the bag so hard, its plastic crinkled. "Beads for Rukku."

"We'll pay you for them by the end of the week," I said.

"Nonsense. It's a gift. Anyway, we'll be gone by the end of the week. I'm glad you visited because I wanted to tell you— we're moving out of the city."

"Moving out?" I echoed. It wasn't like we'd known her that well, but still, she was the only motherly person we'd met in the city. "I'm sorry to hear that, Aunty."

"Don't be sorry. My husband's elder brother wants him to help back in our village, and I'm happy to go."

You sneezed, and at the sound, Teashop Aunty gave us one more gift—a packet of yellow powder.

"Mix some of this in with your milk every day," she advised. "It's a mixture of turmeric and some other medicinal powders. It'll help keep you from falling ill. The monsoon will get worse soon."

"Thanks, Aunty." I didn't bother pointing out that we had no money for milk. We could mix the powder with water instead.

A man's voice called from the front of the shop. Abruptly, Teashop Aunty cut off her chatter. "So nice to see you girls one last time. Good luck."

———

After we left the teashop, you and I wandered along, looking for a place to make your necklaces. Makeshift stalls stocked with fireworks had sprung up along the sidewalks, and seeing them, I realized the Divali festival was coming up.

Divali was your least favorite festival. You hated the noisy celebrations, with people setting off fireworks at every street corner.

We found a park and settled down on a bench under a large tree, whose thick branches gave us some shelter from the drizzle. I found a large plastic bottle and stuck it in the ground, to collect rainwater for us to drink. At least I would have one less worry during the rainy season—we could get our drinking water straight from the sky.

Kutti nosed through a small mound of garbage, searching for a scrap to eat, his coat glistening.

"Rukku," I said, "will you teach me to make necklaces?"

You weren't a good teacher—or maybe I wasn't a good student. I tried watching and imitating what you did, but it took me forever just to string a few beads. Unlike you, I was clumsy with my hands. Beads slipped and rolled away at my touch, and I couldn't make the complicated knots and loops that gave your necklaces a finished look. I was scrabbling around, trying to pick up some beads I'd spilled, when I heard a girl's voice behind me.

"Want this?" A girl stood before us—her school uniform visible beneath her transparent raincoat. A khaki school satchel was hanging off her shoulder.

"Want this?" she repeated, waving a package at us. "Take it. Please?"

I looked at the picture of the pretty orange cream cookies on the cover of the package. If I opened my mouth, I was sure I'd drool worse than Kutti.

"My mother said I mustn't give money to beggars," the girl rattled on. "But she said food was okay."

I scowled at the girl. "Did you hear us beg?"

"No . . ." She knit her brows together. "So you're not beggars, but you're poor, for sure."

I couldn't argue with that.

"Giving food to poor children is a good thing." She smiled, confident and pleased with herself again. "So here are some cookies. For you."

You sneezed, wiped your nose on your sleeve, and continued with your beadwork.

"Come on," the girl coaxed. "Take them."

"Find someone else." I gave her my haughtiest look.

"Please? I need to do one good deed every day, Teacher said, and I didn't get to do one yesterday, and I couldn't lie, and my best friend, Meena, did two yesterday, and if I can't do one today, she'll gloat, so please? Please?"

She looked so desperate, waving that cookie package. She was the begging one, not me.

"Fine," I said.

"Thank you! Thank you!" She shoved the cookies into my hands and darted off.

I turned the cookie package around in my hands, feeling like a princess who'd just granted a favor to a pitiful subject.

27

HUNGRY GHOST

After a while, you'd finished two simple necklaces, and I'd finished a half. We managed to sell one of yours, but for a pitiful sum of money. I tried not to be too disappointed—surely our bead sales would pick up again once we had a bigger stock of necklaces to show.

"Let's head back," I said. "It looks like it's letting up a bit."

Pale sunshine poked through a break in the clouds as we walked back to the graveyard. It hardly ever rained all day and all night, even at the peak of the rainy season. But although the rain had been light, we'd stayed out so long that our clothes were wet through.

I hoped the sun would soon dry us. We had no change of clothes.

At the graveyard, Kutti ran to greet the boys, who were waiting for us.

"Any luck?" I asked.

"Not really," Arul said. "We went all the way to a waste mart I'd seen before, but it's gone—they've bulldozed the slums in that part of the city to build a shopping complex."

"Speaking of building, we found this great place to build a new shelter!" Muthu showed me a grave that was wider than the rest, beneath a banyan tree. "And a nice plastic tablecloth!"

Not so nice, I thought. The tablecloth stank like the garbage they'd rescued it from. The only thing that was great was how cheerful Muthu sounded.

The boys suggested we build a tent around the large grave, using it as the floor of our shelter, because it was raised above the soggy ground. You and Muthu dragged some fallen branches over to use as tent poles. We stuck them as deep into the ground as we could. We used one tarp as our roof, tying its four corners to the tops of the tent pole branches with ropes the boys had scrounged up. Once our roof was up, we pulled the other tarp around the poles, securing it as best we could to make three flimsy walls. We hung the tablecloth across the side that was still open, to make a flappy door.

"We found these three bits of tire, to use as pillows," Arul said. "I don't need one. And later we can get new mats."

As you and Muthu arranged the pieces of tire in our shelter, you doubled over with a coughing fit. I quickly mixed the powder Teashop Aunty had given us with the rainwater I'd collected. Arul and I set a good example by drinking some of the bitter liquid.

But Muthu made a huge fuss. "Tastes worse than poison,"

he sputtered, swallowing it only after I promised to reward him with a cookie.

And I couldn't get you to swallow more than a mouthful. You spat out the first sip and then refused to eat or drink anything else. Not even the bananas Arul had brought or our cookies.

"Can't be good for us," Muthu declared, "if it's made Rukku lose her appetite."

We squeezed into our new sleeping quarters. I was almost happy it was so cramped, because I was grateful for the warmth—our damp clothes made me feel chilly. And because, though I knew Arul was right that we had nothing to fear from the dead, a part of me was still scared a ghost might float by.

Ghosts didn't visit, but swarms of mosquitoes did, feasting on us and droning loudly in our ears.

"Nice lullaby," Muthu said. "When we move out of this place, I'll miss our musical entertainment."

"Tomorrow we'll buy some mosquito repellent," Arul promised.

Too tired to swat at the hungry mosquitoes, I dozed off, only to be wakened by the sound of footsteps. Someone was moving around in the graveyard. Had the waste mart man found us? Or was it a ghost?

I held on to Kutti so he wouldn't give away our hiding place. His hair was on end, and he stood alert.

"There's nothing here." It was a rasping voice I didn't

recognize. A boy. Definitely not the waste mart man. "This place is nice and peaceful and deserted. Now let's go back."

"I'm telling you, this place is haunted," came another boy's voice. "I saw a ghost moving near that banyan tree yesterday evening, when I was cycling by."

Arul sat up. He'd heard the approaching voices, too.

A twig snapped so loudly, it roused you and Muthu.

"Hungry," you moaned. "Hungry."

"Shhh," I whispered. "Shhh, please, Rukku."

"Did you hear that?" a voice said.

I stiffened.

"Didn't hear anything." The other boy was trying to sound nonchalant, but his voice trembled.

"Hungry!" you wailed again. "Hungryyy!"

"Ghost?" the second voice yelped. "Ghost!"

"Hungryyyyyy!" you shrieked. "Hungryyyyy!"

We heard the boys thrashing through the undergrowth, twigs snapping as they rushed away from us through the darkness.

Muthu's shoulders shook with suppressed laughter.

I heard the boys call out for God's protection and dash away, raising a racket as they stumbled through the dark grave-yard.

Muthu couldn't control his laughter anymore. It burst out of him, but he did his best to sound like a demonic villain. Arul and I gave in to our laughter, too.

When we finally stopped roaring, tears were running down my cheeks. By then, you'd tired yourself out.

"Sorry." I hiccupped, finally finding the bananas you'd refused to eat that evening and handing you one. "Those boys were just too funny."

"Great work, Rukku." Arul patted you on the back. "You just made this graveyard even safer than it was before."

"What were they up to?" I said. "Daring each other to explore a 'haunted' graveyard?"

"Rich boys, for sure," Arul said. "You have to be rich to waste time going on escapades at night instead of catching up on precious sleep."

28

◆

DIVALI DUSK

That morning, the three of us brushed our teeth using neem twigs, like Amma said people had done in the old days. The twigs were bitter, so you refused to use them. Plus you were busy sneezing.

"Divali is today and tomorrow," Arul said, "so shops won't be open. No point trying to search for a new waste mart man, but we should still try to collect as much as we can so we'll have a lot to sell by the day after tomorrow."

"Soon," Muthu said confidently, "we'll have tons of stuff, and we'll find a nice new waste mart man who'll give us a lot of money, and we'll buy five packages of those orange cream biscuits—"

"Orange Uncle," you said.

"An uncle who is an orange?" Muthu said. "Can we nibble on him? It'll make a nice change from bananas."

I explained about the gardener who'd thrown an orange at us.

"Let's try our luck there," I suggested. "At least if he chases us away again, we might get another orange."

"Any policemen there?" Muthu wanted to know. "Or watchmen?"

"No, but it was a rich neighborhood, so maybe they'll pay more for Rukku's necklaces."

"Or maybe they got rich by being stingier, so they'll pay less," Muthu said.

———————

The gardener was weeding a flower bed. He glanced up, as though he could feel my eyes on him.

"I see you're back." He wiped his sweaty brow. "And you've found work." Apparently, one look at Arul's sack, not to mention our filthy clothes, showed him we were in the ragpicking business, because he said, "Wait. I'll get you some bottles."

He disappeared around the back of the house and reappeared, carrying a few glass bottles. He was dropping them into Arul's sack when the rich girl bounded out of the house and flounced over to us in her frilly dress.

"Praba, you'll get wet!" Her mother followed her out, unfurling an umbrella.

"Your clothes are so dirty!" Admiration and shock mixed together in Praba's voice. "My mummy would never let me get so dirty."

Kutti jumped up and licked her hands.

"Mummy, he's such a friendly doggie," Praba said. "Please, can I have him?"

"He's ours!" I told her.

"Please, Mummy," the girl wheedled, like she hadn't heard me. Did she think poor, low-caste kids like us didn't count?

"Rich kids," Arul muttered. "Think they can get anything they want."

Kutti shook raindrops off his coat, splattering the mother's sari. She didn't seem to mind. She stooped down to pet him, although she murmured, "We probably shouldn't pet stray dogs, but he can't be dangerous if he's with these children . . ."

Kutti seemed to have taken an instant liking to Praba and her mother, who was now looking Kutti over, thoroughly examining his eyes and even his teeth.

"Skinny, but a healthy coat," she said. "Though he'd probably run away, if we did buy him."

"He's not for sale," I said.

"He won't run away, Mummy." The girl stroked Kutti's muzzle. "I'll brush his coat so it shines like silk and—"

"Kutti, come here." I didn't need to make friends with this silly rich girl. Neither did he. "Now."

To my satisfaction, Kutti obeyed at once, waggling his tail.

"I know you said he wasn't for sale, but as Praba's taken a liking to him . . ." The mother gave me a hesitant smile. "Would you consider parting with him for—let's say, two thousand rupees?"

Two thousand rupees? My head spun just trying to think of that number, with three beautiful, fat zeros behind it.

Not that it mattered. "I told you he wasn't for sale."

"Sure?" the mother said.

"Very," I said.

"Probably for the best," the mother said.

"Mummy, you could vaccinate him," Praba wheedled. "Please, may I get him some food?"

The mother glanced at me.

"Okay," I said. I couldn't deprive Kutti of the chance to taste rich people's food.

The girl scampered back to the house, raindrops dotting her hair like silver beads. You had to have a store of warm, dry clothes to not mind getting so wet.

"We just went shopping for new Divali clothes." The mother gazed at you as you wiped your runny nose on your torn sleeve. "May I offer you some old clothes? And sweets?"

"Yes, ma'am!" Muthu exclaimed, before I had a chance to reply.

"We don't need charity." I glared at him.

"Please accept it as payment for your work," the mother said. "Without your help recycling waste, our environment would be much filthier."

Stunned into silence, I stared at her. I'd never thought of our job as helpful, let alone worthy of payment from rich people. For the first time ever, I felt proud of the work we did.

I'd have liked her better if she hadn't added, "If you change your mind about your dog, let us know."

The drizzle let up long enough for us to shelter behind a rain tree at the end of the avenue and change into our new old clothes. You picked out a red and green skirt. Seeing you dressed in that bright outfit made my mood brighten.

Praba's mother had also given us a raincoat, which I made you wear when the rain began again. I was worried to hear you sniffling worse than the day before.

We walked past knots of people getting ready to set off firecrackers. I wanted to get you back to the graveyard quickly, away from all this. When he heard the first explosion, Kutti whined and tucked his tail between his legs.

But instead of plugging your ears with your fingers and shutting your eyes and cringing, as you used to do whenever firecrackers went off, you handed me your bag of beads and picked up Kutti.

You whispered to Kutti and stroked him until he was calmer. You were so focused on his fear, you didn't seem to mind the noise yourself.

29

GOD'S WORMS

Overnight, it poured, and the graveyard became a swamp.

You were coughing in concert with the buzzing hordes of mosquitoes, and we were all slapping and scratching at our skin. Your skin looked the worst—it wasn't just bumpy with bites, it was dotted with red where you'd scratched so hard, you'd bled.

"Rukku's the sweetest of us all," Muthu said. "That's why the mosquitoes like her best."

"Looks like she really needs a rest." Arul shot me a worried look. "You girls want to stay here this morning?"

"Rukku wants to make necklaces." Your voice was hoarse, but you grabbed your bag of beads and hugged it to your chest. "Rukku wants to help."

We decided we'd set up shop nearby, so you wouldn't have to walk far in the rain.

Slimy pink earthworms covered the sidewalk and the road,

and we tried avoiding them as we walked, but you noticed one get squashed beneath a cyclist's tire.

"Owwa!" You pointed at it and rubbed your arm, like you'd been hurt.

"Yes," I said. "But it's just a worm."

You looked at another squashed worm on the sidewalk.

"*Paavum.*" You laid it gently on your outstretched palm.

"Cheee!" Muthu said. "Put that down, Rukku!"

Kutti nosed your elbow, trying to cheer you up.

"*Ai!*" You pointed at the muddy earth surrounding a tree whose trunk had busted right through the sidewalk. "Look, Viji!"

"Yes, those worms are alive, Rukku."

"Not dead," you remarked.

"Yes," I said. "They're better off there in the mud, for sure."

"*Paavum,*" you repeated.

"That worm's dead, Rukku," I tried to explain. Death was one of those things, like money, that I wasn't sure how well you understood. "It's never going to move again. Ever."

You ran a finger along the dead worm's body, then picked it up again and put it on the earth around the tree.

"I think Rukku's hoping they'll come back to life if she puts them on the earth," Arul said. "After all, the dead ones are only on the road or the sidewalk. You're trying to save them, aren't you, Rukku?"

"Rukku's the best helper." You found another dead worm on the pavement and put it on the earth. "Arul wants to help?"

"Can't, Rukku." He bit his lip, and let a lifeless worm dangle between his fingers before he dropped it on the wet earth. "They're dead. Gone. You can't bring them back to life. None of us can."

You pouted, but refused to stop, transporting a third worm from the gray concrete onto the grassy earth.

"Maybe we're God's worms," Muthu said suddenly.

"What?" Arul glared at him.

"I'm not being disrespectful, boss." Muthu stared at the thickening rain. "God must be so high up, we must look like worms to him. So when we're starving, he probably just feels like we feel when we see a worm die—a little sad, but not much. I guess God feels a little bit sad for us, but not enough to send us all food."

"I'd settle for God sending us a little less rain," I said. "Then we could find our own food. Come on, Rukku. We can't stay here all day."

"Leave her be." Arul crouched down with you, patting your hand as you crooned to the dead worms. "We're not sweet enough to mourn the worms. Someone should."

So we stayed.

A bus careered past and sprayed us with a fountain of rust-brown puddle water, drenching us. My blouse was plastered to my skin. Your new skirt was sopping wet below the raincoat that stretched only to your knees.

You were shivering and coughing, but you started

stringing beads while we sang out, "Bead necklaces, pretty bead necklaces!"

For the first time ever, a few beads rolled off your tired fingers. But you didn't stop until every last bead was gone.

Your busy fingers made so many necklaces, Rukku.

I still have one, the only one we didn't sell, and nights when I just can't get to sleep here, I count the beads on it, like it's my own kind of rosary.

30

◆

MUTHU'S TALE

The money we made selling your necklaces was all we had that day—and it was even less than we'd made last time.

"We should get Rukku some medicine," I said. "And I'm not going one more night without mosquito repellent."

"I'd rather eat well and let the mosquitoes eat well, too," Muthu argued. He wanted to spend every last coin we had on food, but Arul supported me.

We ended up spending half our money on repellent and cough syrup. Which meant we went to bed with half-empty bellies again.

Worse, you wouldn't let me rub the repellent on you properly, because you didn't like the sticky feel of ointment on your skin.

But in spite of the cough syrup, you weren't any better the next morning.

"You two stay and rest," Arul said. "Muthu and I will see if we can sell the bottles the gardener gave us."

The boys set off, and I began telling you your favorite story. Kutti lay close to us, the scent of his wet fur comforting me as much as his warmth.

When I got to the end, about us always being together, you stared off into the distance as though you could see a palace floating in the air. The look in your eyes scared me. I didn't want you traveling all alone to our palace.

I turned over and lay on my elbows and read my book to you until you dozed off. I felt so faint with hunger that it was an effort just to reread the pages while I waited for the boys' return.

"Bananas!" Muthu's cry woke you.

We crept out of the shelter.

"We found a new waste mart man, but he's worse than stingy." Arul's forehead was scrunched up in a worried frown. "He drove a really hard bargain. Gave us next to nothing for all that glass. It's a good thing Rukku's favorite food is cheap."

When Muthu saw no response from you to your favorite food, he clapped his hands in mock joy. "Bananas, Rukku! It's so long since we last had any! I've forgotten how good they taste!" He bit one, swallowed it right away without even seeming to chew it, and let out a full-throated belch. "See? Is that a miracle or what? We can burp, though we've eaten next to nothing. Now do you believe in God, Akka?"

I laughed, though I was worried about you not eating.

And even Arul laughed, instead of telling Muthu he was going to hell.

That was a miracle.

That evening your skin was warm to the touch, and I was overcome with guilt. I'd come to the city hoping for a better life. As soon as you were better, I needed to do more than just dream about finding a school where we could both study. The closest we'd come to that was meeting that kind woman at church. I'd thrown away the card she'd given me, but the address had stuck in my brain.

"Maybe we should go see the lady we met in church—Celina Aunty—tomorrow," I said. "We could go to school and—"

"School?" Muthu sputtered. "No way!"

"Why shouldn't we see what she has to offer?"

"That woman is a liar," Muthu cried.

"No she isn't. She told the priest we weren't thieves, remember?"

"Why?" Muthu demanded. "Why should a well-dressed woman care enough to argue with a priest for the sake of kids she doesn't know?"

"Because she's good?"

"Because she's trying to catch us and sell us," Muthu said.

"Don't be ridiculous."

"You're the one being ridiculous," he said. "I went to one of those 'schools' once. It was a prison."

"What?"

Arul put his arm around Muthu. "You don't have to tell."

"I must," Muthu said. "Akka needs to know."

"Know what?" I was scared to ask. Muthu's tone was so serious, so different from usual.

You and Kutti sensed the change in him, too. You touched his cheek with a tired hand. Kutti shifted his position and laid his head on Muthu's lap.

"I was sold to a 'school' once," Muthu said. "A school where they 'taught' us to make handbags. We had to cut and sew all day. They kept us locked in. The man who called himself our owner only let us go to the bathroom at dawn and at night after our work was done. To eat, we only got stale rotis—if we were lucky."

I shivered, but from the coldness of his voice, not the damp, chilly air.

"If we didn't finish as many handbags as he demanded, or didn't do whatever he said we must, he lashed us with his leather belt until we bled."

I took one of Muthu's palms in my own, but he didn't respond to my touch. His mind seemed far away.

"One day," Muthu continued, "police raided the place and took us to an orphanage. But the woman at the orphanage was a rakshasi." He shuddered. "A demon. She beat us, too. Not as bad as the man, but bad enough that I ran away."

"I found him," Arul said, picking up where Muthu had left off, "hiding behind a garbage can. We shared some food, and by the next morning . . ."

"I was helping you," Muthu finished. "You became my boss."

"Not boss," Arul said. "Brother."

"No." Muthu was firm.

"If Viji can be your sister, why can't I—"

"Boss is better," Muthu said. "My stepbrother's the one who sold me."

Arul looked so upset, I knew it was the first time he'd heard that part of Muthu's story.

Listening to the rain plinking against the gravestones, I stared at our tarp roof that was swaying in the strengthening wind. Muthu's tale had horrified me, but I wasn't sure he was right about Celina Aunty.

My back hadn't felt like a snake was crawling up it when I'd met Celina Aunty, like I'd felt with the creepy waste mart man and the nasty bus driver. If anything, she seemed unusually kind.

But could I really trust my feelings? I hadn't been on my own as long as Arul and Muthu—surely they knew this world better than I did.

31

◆

FEVER

All through that starless night, your breath came in wheezy gasps as raindrops wriggled, like silver snakes, through the gaps in our tent.

When I rubbed mosquito repellent on your skin, your eyelids fluttered open, but you were too tired to shove me away.

I would have given anything to see you throw a tantrum or complain.

I mashed a bit of the last blackened, limp banana between my fingers, and you swallowed a few small bites. Then you sipped some water.

Before I could rejoice, thinking you were on the mend, you clutched at your stomach, crawled a few feet away, retched, and threw up.

Muthu stirred awake, and his eyes had a glazed, feverish look. "Look at him," I said to Arul. "Now Muthu's ill, too."

"I'm just too full to move after that fine meal we had last night," Muthu joked, though his voice was softer than usual.

"You three stay here," Arul said. "I'll work alone today."

"One person can't make enough to feed four mouths even on a good day," I said. "I'll go."

I'd never left you with anyone else before, but we had no choice. Muthu was shivering. He definitely needed rest.

"What, Akka?" Muthu said. "You're missing the fresh air around the dumps so much, you want to work today?"

I forced a smile. "When Rukku's better, we'll start up the necklace business again, and then we'll make enough money so we can take a holiday and both of you can just play together for a whole week."

"No, no, Akka." Muthu grinned weakly at me. "If you kept me from working that long, I'd fall ill from shock."

Arul's face was too grimly set to smile.

Arul led me to a lot between two tumbledown houses where people had thrown trash after the holiday. Gullies of water ran down the sides of the enormous garbage pile, into an ocean of water that looked and smelled like raw sewage. Useless burned-out fireworks bobbed in it, but I spotted a precious bottle poking out of the trash mound.

I bunched up my skirt, tied the hem around my waist, and waded through the water toward the bottle.

A while later, Kumar and two of the boys in his gang joined us.

"Where's that brat Sridar so I can stay away from him?" I craned my neck, searching for the rude boy.

"He's gone," Kumar said.

"Gone?" I echoed. "Happy to hear it. Gone where?"

"Dead," Kumar said.

"Dead! I—I thought—"

"Thought he went on holiday?" Kumar gave a bitter laugh. "He got sick from something. Kept vomiting and then . . ."

"I am so sorry." I looked down at the gray sludge into which my feet had sunk. "I am really, really sorry."

"Don't be." Kumar churned the filthy water with his stick. "Kids die every day. You start feeling sorry, you'll drown."

From what I'd seen of him, Sridar was selfish and mean. Still, he didn't deserve to die so young. It shocked me that someone like us could be here one day—and dead the next.

Arul put an arm around Kumar's shoulder. For a long moment, they stood together, still as gravestones, any rivalry forgotten.

Then they moved apart, and we went to work, trying to dredge out at least a few bottles or tins from the sea of sewage.

32

THE PRICE OF FREEDOM

Thunder boomed. Purple rain clouds burst over us like rotting grapes.

"You'd better see how Rukku and Muthu are doing," Arul said. "I'll sell what we've found."

Sheets of rain blinded me as I hurried to the graveyard. In spite of how brave you'd been with Kutti during Divali, I was scared I'd find you cowering with fear when I returned.

What I found was even scarier.

Your body was a tight knot. You lips twitched, but no sound escaped them. Your forehead was hot, and your hair was mangled with sweat.

Kutti was pacing about restlessly, as if he understood you weren't well and it upset him as much as it upset me.

"Her fever's worse, I think," Muthu said. His own eyes still had a feverish glaze.

"Rest. I'll look after you both."

Muthu fell into an exhausted sleep.

I dipped our towel in cool rainwater and squeezed it over your eyes, but your forehead stayed burning hot. I dripped water past your lips—every time I could. I lost track of how many desperate hours went by.

The wind picked up. It tore away the plastic tablecloth we'd used as a door and sent it flapping like a bat across the dark graveyard. Kutti and I raced after it. I pinned it down, but only after it was nearly torn in two. Struggling against the wind and lashing rain, I tied the ragged pieces as best I could across the gap, but everything inside was already wet. A rash had broken out on your back, making your skin as rough as sandpaper, and you moaned every now and then.

Muthu slept on, not waking even when Arul staggered into our storm-ravaged shelter without money and with hardly any more food.

"I ran into a nasty gang," he said. "They stole our stuff and shoved me into a gutter. But thankfully they didn't beat me up."

All we had for dinner was what he'd been able to scrounge out of the garbage: a tin of some yellow-green slop, two rotting bananas, and some moldy rotis. But hunger was clawing so fiercely at my stomach that I shut my eyes, scooped up a handful of the swill, and stuck it in my mouth.

"Let's save the fruit for Rukku and Muthu," Arul suggested.

I scraped off the green fuzz growing on a roti. We ate in

silence, broken only by your labored breaths and the rainstorm lashing the banyan's branches.

Our bellies were empty, but I was used to that. Now I also felt empty of hope.

I hardly slept, and when dawn came, I knew I needed to make a plan.

Somehow, I had to find a way to get money. I needed to buy you good food, medicine for your fever, and things to shore up our shelter and make it comfortable.

A thought entered my mind as I stroked Kutti. I pushed it away. But it returned.

I didn't want to. I had no right to. I couldn't do it.

I could.

I had to.

While you three continued to sleep, I led Kutti out of the graveyard. We walked toward the part of town where the rich girl lived.

My feet felt heavy as sacks full of scrap metal. And it wasn't just my feet that dragged. It was like my mind was dragging my heart along, and it and the rest of my body didn't want to come.

When I reached the gate with Goddess Lakshmi's name on it, I knelt on the wet sidewalk and hugged Kutti close. "Kutti, I have to help my sister and Muthu. This is the only way. Do you understand?"

He stared straight into my eyes. His tail didn't wag.

"I'm sorry, Kutti. I'm really, really sorry."

I'm not sure how long I clung to him, rubbing my forehead against his rain-plastered neck and breathing the scent of his wet fur. He nudged me with his warm nose, like he wanted to comfort me, but it only made me hurt worse.

Somehow, I forced myself to clang on the gate.

The gardener opened it. "You again? What do you want?"

"I'm here to sell our dog," I said.

"Can't wake them at the crack of dawn," he grumbled, but I pushed past him, strode down the drive, and rapped hard on the front door.

A maid opened it and would have slammed the door in my face, except that the mother of the girl was close behind.

"Yes?" the mother said.

"Kutti—our dog," I said. "I'm here to sell him. Two thousand rupees, you told me."

"Praba will be thrilled. She really fell in love with him."

I knelt and pressed my face against Kutti's warm neck one last time.

"Go in, Kutti." Gently, I pushed him. "This is your new home."

He cocked his head, like you did when you were listening hard. I knew he was trying to understand.

"You're a smart dog, Kutti. A good dog. We have to give you away, though. For Rukku. Understand?"

He whined. I gave him another gentle shove.

"You'll like this place. Stay here."

The mother rustled off and returned with money and a package. "Here's money and some food. And he'll be happy here, I promise," she said.

My eyes were blinded with tears, and I couldn't thank her.

Without saying another word, I turned around and walked away.

Kutti tried to follow. I heard him yowl, heard his toes clip-clopping on the floor as he struggled to break free before the door slammed behind me.

33

LIES

The pharmacist sold me blister packs of pills to soothe pain, bring down fever, and help you sleep.

"You need to see a doctor if someone in your family's got a fever," he warned. "There's a bad illness going around."

He was trying to be kind, I could tell. I almost asked him if he knew a good doctor or a good hospital.

Then I remembered how Amma had shielded you from doctors and hospitals. I hadn't come so far with you to risk having strangers snatch you away and lock you in an institution forever.

———

On the way to the graveyard, I stopped to buy two new tarps, one to lay across our tent so we could keep dry again and another for a better door. Praba's mother had given us perfectly good bananas and bags of banana chips, but from a nearby stall, I bought a doll with bright black hair you could comb. Then, as I hurried back, I dreamed of how I'd spend the rest of our money later, on things that would make our life more comfortable, starting with a foam mattress for you and Muthu, and new books for me to read to everyone.

Arul was looking for me when I returned.

"I was worried sick!" Arul scolded. "What happened?"

"Kutti's gone." I thrust all the remaining money into his hands.

"You—sold . . ." Arul didn't seem to be able to finish the sentence.

At least I didn't have to explain.

"Rukku won't really mind," I tried to convince myself. "She had a doll she used to love, so I got her this, see . . ."

Arul didn't say anything. He didn't frown and didn't smile either.

"Rukku?" I shook you gently. "I have medicine. And fresh bananas." I waved a bright yellow one under your nose.

You were unusually docile, swallowing the medicine without any argument.

"Kutti?" Your eyes searched the tent.

"Kutti's gone," I said.

"Gone?" you echoed.

"Who's gone?" Muthu opened his eyelids slowly and sat up.

"Kutti left." I had thought of saying Kutti was run over by a truck, but what if Muthu asked to bury the body?

"Can't be," Muthu protested. "He's never run off before."

"Maybe he just didn't like living here in the graveyard." The more I said, the less convincing my lie sounded. "He's gone, I'm telling you. Gone."

"Dogs don't just go away," Muthu said.

"How do you know? You've had dogs before, or what?"

"He loved us." Muthu's confidence was unshakable.

"He's just a dog, not a human being! Even humans leave people they love!"

"Dogs are loyal," Muthu said.

"Maybe Kutti wanted a better life, so he left."

For the first time since you'd fallen ill, you seemed to be following a conversation. I felt triumphant, as if the medicine was already working, although I knew no medicine worked right away.

"Enough about Kutti. I bought medicine for you both. Rukku's had hers. Now you."

"Thanks, Akka," Muthu whispered. "My head hurts. And my joints and my bones and even behind my eyes. I'm hurting all over."

"You'll be better tomorrow," Arul said. "Once the medicine starts working."

I was sure I'd done the right thing until you murmured, "Kutti left."

The quiet acceptance in your tone jolted me, and I wondered if my lie about Kutti not loving us enough to stay had hurt you worse than if I'd pretended he'd died.

It sounded like you'd given up altogether. On him, on me, on everything.

34

THE COURAGE TO TRUST

As the day wore on, I told myself your fever was coming down, that the medicines were allowing you to sleep more deeply, that you'd be better when you woke.

But that night, I couldn't pretend anymore. We couldn't deny you were worse.

Although we had better food than ever, I couldn't get you to eat or drink. I couldn't even get you to open your eyes.

I drew your head onto my lap and stroked your brow. I called your name.

You didn't respond at all.

"It's not true, Rukku," I confessed in my desperation. "I sold Kutti, even though he was more yours than mine. I'm so sorry. I only wanted to save you, Rukku. Get better. Please."

By then, I don't think you could hear me.

"Maybe we should light a candle in church for them?" Arul suggested.

"Or maybe we should ask the woman we met in church for help," I said.

Arul wound your new doll's hair around one of his wrists like a handcuff.

"I don't see any other way, Arul."

"But don't you remember what Muthu said?"

"What would you rather do? Watch them—watch them . . ." I couldn't finish the sentence.

When I think of it now, it seems so clear, so simple that I should have gone straight to Celina Aunty once your fever spiked. But I was so terribly confused, Rukku.

Only a few adults had ever really helped us. And this was more than just seeking help. This was trusting her—a stranger—completely.

"Well, she was in church and did seem kind," Arul said softly, as if to convince himself this was the right thing to do.

"Let's go." I repeated the address that I remembered on the card.

"Not too far." Arul gathered your limp body in his arms. "Can you help Muthu get there?"

Muthu's lids drooped when I woke him. He didn't seem to know or care what was happening, because without argument, he let me slide an arm beneath his shoulders and drag him along, half asleep.

Through needles of rain, we staggered toward the home for

children that Muthu had been so sure was a kind of jail. Frayed yellow threads of dawn were trailing through the sky when we finally reached the gate.

It was locked.

"Help!" I shook it until it jangled loudly, and a woman came out.

Celina Aunty.

35

◆

HOSPITAL

"Can you help my sister?" I asked Celina Aunty. I thrust our money into her hands. "We can pay."

"Of course I'll help." Celina Aunty took the money. "And. I'll keep this safe for you."

"I'm not coming," Arul muttered.

"Your choice." Celina Aunty took Rukku's limp body from Arul. "We don't force anyone to live here."

Inside, Celina Aunty laid Rukku down on a sofa and motioned for me to set Muthu down on another. "I have to call a doctor. They need to go to a hospital."

"Promise you won't lock my sister away?" The old fear surged inside me again.

"I'd never do that."

Celina Aunty spoke to a doctor on the phone and waited with me until she came. The doctor took your temperature and listened to your chest. You didn't shrink from her gentle touch and kind voice.

She examined Muthu next, but I only had eyes for you.

Dr. Sumitra asked me lots of questions: "Did you use mosquito nets?" "Did you boil the water before you drank it?" "What medication did you try to give her?" "How much?" "How long has her brow felt so hot?"

As best I could, I answered those questions.

When I asked the only question that mattered to me— "Will my sister be okay?"—Dr. Sumitra didn't reply.

She left to join Celina Aunty in the next room, where they spoke in hushed tones. I strained my ears but couldn't catch what they were saying.

In that room where you were lying, a cross hung on the wall above the sofa, like the one we'd seen in church. Looking at Yesu on the cross, I said the prayer Arul had taught me. I said every prayer Amma had sung that I could remember. I prayed silently, words echoing in my head louder than anything I'd ever spoken.

Wherever you are, I begged, *whoever you are, please, let Rukku get better.*

It must only have been a few minutes later that men came and carried you and Muthu into an ambulance. Celina Aunty and I got in. You were both in such a stupor that neither the flashing lights nor the sirens seemed to upset you.

The men carried the two of you into a hospital. Silent as a shadow, I followed Celina Aunty while she talked to people and filled out forms, and the men wheeled you both out of sight.

A strangely familiar scent rose from the floor. After all those days of having my nose filled with the scents of rubbish, it took me time to recognize the burning scent of the acrid liquid Amma used to clean our bathroom every once in a while.

Celina Aunty tried to explain. "Dr. Sumitra thinks they may have dengue fever. It's carried by mosquitoes."

"They'll get better, right?"

"I hope so, Viji. Most people do, but . . ." Her eyes got shiny like she was about to cry.

She clutched my hand until a nurse came and led us through the hospital to peek into the overcrowded ward where you were. You and Muthu lay in beds near one another. You were each hooked up to a contraption that dripped medicine and food and water into your veins, Celina Aunty explained.

"They'll be well looked after," she promised.

She didn't promise you'd get better.

———————————

I wanted to stay with you, but Celina Aunty insisted the best thing I could do was try to get some sleep and make sure I didn't fall ill, too.

Back at the home, she asked questions about us.

We'd always looked out for each other, I said. I told her how you'd earned money with your beadwork, how well you could work with your hands, how most of our teachers and even Amma thought you couldn't do much of anything.

At that, she frowned. "Too often, we expect too little," she said.

"Rukku was more careful about what she ate than we were. She never waded through trash like we did," I said. "It's not fair she fell ill."

"Life isn't fair." Celina Aunty sighed. "There are too many children like you without a home. And children shouldn't have to work. I'm just glad I can help you a little now. Thank you for trusting me, Viji."

If only I'd trusted Celina Aunty sooner, you and Muthu might have been playing in the sunshine, celebrating the end of the rainy season, instead of lying on hospital beds.

That night, Celina Aunty asked if I wanted to call anyone on the phone or write anyone a letter.

I wrote to Amma, but I didn't tell Celina Aunty whom I was writing to.

I let Amma know we were in the city with good friends. I asked her if she was all right, said I would earn and send her money.

I didn't tell her how sick you were.

I didn't want to believe it.

36

GONE

I ate and slept, but hardly spoke to the other girls in my room or to the boys who slept in another part of the house.

After breakfast, Celina Aunty drove me from the house where she lived, along with two teachers and all the children, to the hospital.

There, I held your hand and told you our story, although you slept the whole time.

Muthu was delirious, raving in his sleep.

The doctor confirmed you both had dengue fever. Except you had developed pneumonia, too. Muthu hadn't, so his condition was less complicated.

A night or two later, Dr. Sumitra proclaimed that Muthu was "out of danger," and he was sent to another part of the hospital.

When I saw him—scrubbed clean by a nurse, with his hair

cut short and washed and brushed—I could hardly believe it was Muthu. I realized I must have looked more presentable, too, because Celina Aunty had given me clothes, and I'd bathed and combed my hair. But Muthu didn't comment on my appearance.

He just asked, "How's Rukku?"

"Not well enough," I said.

He slipped his fingers through mine. They felt bony as a skeleton's.

"Will you tell me the story, Akka?" he asked. "The fairy tale you used to tell on the bridge?"

I tried a few times but kept choking up, unable to get beyond the first sentences.

"Never mind." Muthu squeezed my hand tight.

That afternoon, a surprise was waiting for me.

Arul.

"I couldn't stand being away," Arul said. "I'd rather be locked in with all of you than alone and free."

His words felt like a warm ray of sunshine slipping in through a rain-soaked sky.

Arul had brought with him the new doll I'd bought you. The one you'd been too sick to play with.

When we visited you that night, I took the doll with us, hoping your eyes would light up when you saw her.

But by the time we stood by your bed, your own body was as stiff as a wooden doll's and it was too late.

Celina Aunty asked many questions. Hadn't I written a letter to someone? Were our parents alive? Shouldn't she try to contact them?

No, I said. Definitely not.

What should she do with your body?

I didn't reply.

Burned or buried, what was the difference? You were gone.

Arul answered for me. He said you were Christian, so we should bury you. And I thought of you lighting candles and didn't say no.

Christmas came about a month after your funeral. The rains had stopped by then.

In the hall of the home, Celina Aunty set up a little crèche, a set of dolls in a stable: baby Yesu, Mary, Joseph, three kings, a drummer boy, and lots of animals. Outside the front door, she hung a paper star with a twinkling light inside. You'd have loved all of this—as well as the strings of lights she wound around the crèche and the branch she stuck in a pot and called a Christmas tree.

She gave all of us presents. The little kids who live at the home laughed and gave me friendly smiles, but it was hard for me to act like I was in good spirits.

Arul and Muthu got fancy kurtas, which they changed into right away. I noticed they had both put on a bit of weight. But though Muthu's body looked less frail than before, his eyes hadn't regained their twinkle. And he wasn't the chatterbox you knew either. He was unusually quiet around me, like he knew I couldn't stand it if he started making jokes.

"You look smart in your new clothes," I managed to say.

"What did you get, Akka?" Muthu asked.

I didn't care what my gift was, but I opened the package, for his sake.

I got a notebook, handmade paper, and pencils made from recycled scraps.

"What's this for?" Muthu asked.

"To write on," Celina Aunty said.

"I have no one to write to and nothing to say," I told her.

She didn't respond. Not right away. But before we went to bed that night, Celina Aunty called me into the schoolroom and motioned me toward one of the empty desks.

"Sit," she ordered. "Write."

"Write?" I said. "Why?"

"Because you're not talking much to anyone, Viji, and that's not healthy. Your thoughts are sitting inside you like a stone, and I think you should set them down on paper."

I stared at the empty page before me and picked up the pencil, and she corrected my grip, and I stared at the page some more.

The paper seemed to stretch. Its emptiness grew, and mine grew, too. My fingers went limp, and the pencil rolled off onto the floor.

She picked up the pencil and put it in my hands again.

For months, I couldn't write, Rukku. Celina Aunty would sit beside me, reading, keeping me silent company.

Arul and Muthu visited your grave in a nearby cemetery every week and laid flowers on it.

I didn't join them.

But I did all the chores I was supposed to do at the home. In fact, I liked doing chores, not only because it made me feel like I was not living on charity, but also because it gave me a reason to do something when I felt like a rock was sitting on my chest, weighing me down so I couldn't rise out of bed.

GOOD IS GOD

During the day, students of all ages sit together in the biggest room in the house, learning. Reading, writing, mathematics, history, geography, science. The teachers give us different things to do, and we work at our own pace.

Arul doesn't join us, because he has no interest in schoolwork. Instead, he takes a bus every morning to work with a carpenter. Celina Aunty says this is an important path, too—getting special skills to become carpenters, tailors, gardeners, or to learn some other trade.

She says she wishes she had more space, so she could take in every homeless kid, but she can't. She doesn't have enough space for all of us to live here forever, so those who are older, like me and especially like Arul, who's even a bit older, are allowed to stay for a bit, until we have a safe, sure place to move to.

Before our lessons each morning, we gather in the hall to

pray. Most of the children here are Christian, like Celina Aunty, but some are Hindu, and two are Muslims.

The prayer assembly is unending. Celina Aunty starts off with Arul's favorite prayer to "our father" and then there are prayers to Mary and Allah, and some Hindu chants that Amma used to say. When I hear those, I miss Amma.

It amazes me that there are so many different words to pray with, and so many people praying, but there is still so much misery and cruelty in the world.

This morning, during the prayer assembly, I yawned and yawned, and Muthu caught my eye and started yawning, too. Soon, I'd set the whole place yawning.

Priya Aunty, one of our other teachers, told me off. "You're the oldest girl here," she said. "If you don't start showing respect, all the little ones are going to behave badly."

"I don't behave badly," I said.

"Don't talk back." Her face flushed redder than a brick. Lips quivering with rage, she hauled me off to Celina Aunty's office and ranted. Celina Aunty listened and didn't let me say a word until after Priya Aunty stormed off into the classroom.

"Viji, I can imagine you feel guilty about your sister's death, but you need to stop accusing yourself. You made the choices that seemed best. You did all you could."

Those weren't the words I'd expected from her.

"Religion can be a solace, Viji. If you have faith in a higher power, if you trust that each life has a purpose whether we see it or not, if you could only believe your sister has a soul that's still alive—"

"You want to convert me? You can't," I told her. "Ask Arul. He's been trying ever since we met."

"I'm not trying and never will try to convert you, Viji. It's just that when we suffer a loss like you have, we lose a sense of purpose. I lost hope when I lost my husband, and I found it again in God, but it's not the only way. Maybe your way is to search inside yourself and rediscover purpose."

My life felt pointless now that you were gone. She got that right, but I didn't say so.

"You also need to respect Priya Aunty's position," she said quietly. "We can't have children here being disrespectful to any religion."

"I'm not mean about any one religion," I said. "They're all equally silly."

An amused smile flickered across her face. "We can't have you being disrespectful to all religions either."

What about respecting my nonreligion? I thought.

As though I'd spoken those words, Celina Aunty said, "I think I understand you, Viji."

She wrote two words on a piece of paper and turned it toward me so I could read them.

God and *Good*, side by side.

"Those two words, *God* and *Good*, are only one letter apart in the English language," she said. "So maybe, when we pray in the morning, if you don't want to think of God, you might try thinking about being Good. About doing Good. Yes?"

"Okay," I said.

"I don't mind if you have no faith in religion, Viji. Just as long as you have faith in the goodness within yourself."

39

◆

LOSING AND FINDING

Celina Aunty assigned me and Arul the job of doing the dishes together. For months, we didn't talk much as we worked side by side in the kitchen. But one evening, Arul finally broke the silence.

He asked how I was doing, and when, as usual, I just said, "Fine," he wouldn't let me get away with it.

"No," he said. "You're not fine, Viji."

I said nothing.

"Talk to me," he said. "Let me help."

"I don't need your help," I growled.

Arul sighed. "Sulking and being rude to people who care about you isn't going to make life any easier."

"Since when," I said, "has life been easy?"

"Since now!" Arul let a dish clatter into the sink. "Some

things are easier here than on the bridge—in spite of all that's happened—and you have to stop feeling sorry for yourself."

"I don't just sulk!" I shocked myself by shouting for the first time since your passing. "I do every chore I'm given. I clean. I sit in the classroom. I eat. I sleep."

"You don't look like you've been sleeping much."

"That's because Rukku is gone, Arul! She's gone because of me. If I hadn't forced her to leave home—"

"If she hadn't come here with you, she'd never have enjoyed the good times we had, and we had so many good times, Viji."

"I should never have run away."

"What choice did you have? I've heard of parents who beat their kids to death. Who knows what your father might have done? You tried your best—"

"It's my fault Rukku died."

"Your fault you couldn't see into the future? If you're to blame, we are, too. If I'd believed you when you were scared the waste mart man would come after us, we might never have been forced to live in that mosquito-infested graveyard. If Muthu hadn't scared you off from Celina Aunty, you might have come here sooner."

He couldn't comfort me. I banged the pan against the sink. "I want her back!"

"Stop it." Arul yanked the pan out of my hands. "I miss her, too. So does Muthu."

"She was not your sister! She was mine. Mine. Now I have no one."

"You're no more alone than Muthu and I are," Arul yelled. "If you choose to drown in loneliness, go ahead, but don't claim she wasn't our sister. We're not just friends, we're family."

The loudness of his tone shocked me.

"Start looking at what you haven't lost," Arul said. "Start giving thanks for what you do have."

"Thanks?" An odd snort left my lips. "That's all you ever do. If someone came to stab you, you'd probably thank them, too, wouldn't you? But there's nothing to be thankful about."

"Yes there is," he said, taking my soapy hands in his. "You're here in this home with a chance to do something more with your life. You have Celina Aunty. You have me. You have Muthu. Most of all, you have yourself."

"Myself?"

"Yes. And now that you've been angry and raised your voice again, you'll feel a lot better—just wait and see."

He was right.

When I left the kitchen that night, I found I actually wanted to write to you for the first time.

———

Easter came, and I finally agreed to visit your grave with Arul and Muthu. On your stone, instead of flowers, I laid down one of the chocolate Easter eggs Celina Aunty had given us.

"She'd have loved that," Muthu said. "Sweet, gooey, and wrapped in green foil, her favorite color."

"I'm sure she'd have loved the flowers you always leave for her, too," I said.

As we left the cemetery where you'd been buried, Arul said Easter was about new beginnings. But some things will never change, Rukku.

You'll never be back.

40

—◆—

HOPE

"I'm going to visit a place I'd love for you to see," Celina Aunty told me the next day. "So you're excused from attending lessons."

I shrugged like it didn't matter one way or another, but I felt myself flush with pleasure. She'd chosen me to go somewhere with her, as a special treat.

She drove us to a white bungalow, three stories high, an oasis of calm in the midst of all the noise and bustle. Celina Aunty smiled as she parked the car. "This is a school for children like Rukku."

"Children like Rukku?" Anger spurted out of me. "No one's like Rukku!" I yelled. "No one!"

"Viji? I put that very badly." Celina Aunty bit her lip. "There's no one in the world like your sister. I didn't mean those words to sound the way they did. I'm sorry."

I screwed up my eyelids, tight, so no tears would fall out.

"I have a sister, Viji. A sister with a disability."

My eyes flew open.

"We never were as poor as the two of you, but we weren't rich either. She came to this school. It's a school for young people with intellectual and developmental disabilities."

For a while I said nothing, but her words were a key, opening my locked heart. "Where's your sister now, Celina Aunty?"

"She works at a print shop. She used to have her own little place at the other end of the city, but recently she got married and moved farther away. We meet as often as we can."

"Will you take me to see your sister sometime?"

"Sure. Now, are you ready to go in, Viji?"

"Yes. And I'm sorry for yelling."

Everyone in the building greeted us with smiles and vanakkams. Everyone seemed to know—and like—Celina Aunty.

We were shown into an office. Sitting behind a desk, beneath a picture of the Hindu God Ganesha, was a wiry young woman. She sprang up and pressed her palms together in greeting.

"Viji, this is the director," Celina Aunty said. "Dr. Dhanam."

"Call me Dhanam Aunty, Viji. Come. Let me show you around."

We followed Dhanam Aunty into a sunny, high-ceilinged room. We stayed by the door, peeking in.

A boy around my age was sprawled across the floor, drawing on a large sheet of paper. A little girl of maybe seven or eight was playing with colored blocks. In the center of the room, a few children of all ages sat on straw mats on the floor listening to a silver-haired teacher who sat cross-legged, reading aloud from a picture book. Some of the children looked up at us curiously.

You could have been among them. You could have been here, at this school, learning from teachers who'd pay proper attention to you. A silent flood of tears rushed down my cheeks.

No one seemed to notice I was crying, except the girl with blocks, who marched over to me.

"Don't cry," she commanded. "Come and play with me."

"Thanks," I said to her, trying to swallow my sobs and hold my voice steady. "I'll come and play for a bit."

"Why are you thanking me?" Her forehead wrinkled in confusion. "I didn't give you anything."

"I was sad. You made me feel better."

"I made you better?" Her face glowed like a moon, and her plump cheeks dimpled. "I made her better," she announced to Dhanam Aunty. "Who is she, anyway?"

"This is Viji," Celina Aunty said.

"I'm Lalitha. Come." Lalitha took me by the hand and led me to a shelf full of painting supplies.

"Let's paint," she decided. "We must put newspaper on the floor so it doesn't get messy."

The two of us spread out the paper, and we started working. At least, I did. Lalitha selected a brush and chewed on its end thoughtfully.

I dipped my brush in the paint and tried to draw a yellow

circle for the sun. Lalitha was watching, which made me nervous, because I wasn't the best painter.

The lines I drew for the sun's rays came out pretty wobbly. I dropped a bit of blue paint on the bottom by accident, so I smeared it and made a river. Across it, I painted a bridge. On the bridge I painted four stick figures.

"What's that?" Lalitha put her finger on one of the figures.

"A person," I said.

"You are a person. I am a person." She wagged her finger at me. "That is not a person."

"It's the best I can do. What are you going to paint?"

"I can paint well," Lalitha said. "Watch." She swished her brush around on the paper, making a great yellow blob in the top right corner.

"Is that the sun?" I asked.

"No, Viji. The sun is outside. This is just a big yellow dot."

"Right." I smiled.

So we painted dots and lines and all kinds of shapes. We made a mess and had just as much fun cleaning up, skating on the wet floor after we'd mopped.

"That was the best painting class ever," I told Lalitha when it was time for me to leave. "Thanks."

"Come back," she said. "I'll teach you some more."

On the way home, I asked Celina Aunty, "Can I go back there again? Maybe work at the school?"

"Sure," Celina Aunty said. "I may be able to arrange for you to assist the teachers when they need an extra hand. Maybe help with reading or writing or art? And maybe someday you could even teach there."

Since you'd gone, I hadn't given a thought to my dream of becoming a teacher. Celina Aunty's words made my dream glimmer again. Faint and far away, but not lost.

41

◆

BRIDGES

"Let's go for a walk," Arul said when he returned from his lessons at the carpentry shop that afternoon.

"Can't." Muthu scowled. "I have to write *I won't be rude to my teachers* one hundred times."

"Why?" Arul said. "What did you do?"

"This morning, Priya Aunty said, if a fruit vendor asks us for twenty rupees and we give him a fifty-rupee note, what would we have left? And I said it was a silly question, because if a vendor asks us for twenty, I wouldn't give him fifty, I'd bargain him down, not give more than he asks! And she got mad, but I said it was just as important to learn how to bargain as it was to learn subtraction. All the other kids agreed with me, but that only made her madder, and she gave me extra homework."

Arul started lecturing Muthu on staying out of trouble, but I grinned at Muthu. It was good to know he was getting his spark back.

When I recognized where Arul was heading, I stopped, but he wouldn't let me turn around.

Soon, we arrived at the fancy house where Kutti lived. He was out in the yard.

Kutti's coat shone with cleanliness, sparkling in the sunshine like a silk sari. We watched him through the gate, playing with the girl. The gardener was nowhere to be seen.

Praba threw a ball, and he leaped and caught it midair. She patted him, and he licked her hand, looking at her the way he used to look at you.

"What's the point of this trip?" I said to Arul. "To show me Kutti doesn't miss Rukku anymore?"

Before I could stomp off in a huff, Kutti raised his head and galloped toward the gate, barking madly, his tail wagging so fast, it almost disappeared from view.

Praba ran after him, and when she saw us, she swung the gate open. Kutti bounded over, placed his paws on my knees, and pushed me off balance. He'd grown so much larger and stronger. We collapsed together, his tail thumping me.

"Viji!" The girl surprised me by remembering my name. "You don't look nearly as scruffy as you did last time." She sounded disappointed. "What happened?"

"Changed my line of work," I said.

"Where's Rukku?" she said.

"Couldn't come." I buried my face in Kutti's fur. He smelled clean and fresh.

"Want to see the bed I made for Kutti in my room?" Praba asked. "I give him dog biscuits every day, and I wash him once a week with special dog shampoo—"

"Dog shampoo?" They not only had special biscuits for dogs, but even special shampoo?

"Come on," she said. "I'll show you."

"We don't have time now," I said, because I was afraid her mother might not want me in her house, even though she was kind and I was a lot cleaner than I had been. And it was enough to see that Kutti was doing well.

Kutti put a paw on my foot, like he was telling me to stay. But I scratched Kutti behind the ears and got up.

"Go, Kutti," I said. "Go on home."

"When will you visit again?" Praba asked.

"Sometime," Arul said. "Sure."

As we walked away, Kutti gave a little whine, but he didn't try to follow. He knew where he belonged now.

"I thought you would like to see how happy Kutti is," Arul said.

"You've visited him before?" I asked.

"Just once," Arul said. "Long enough to show me two things, Viji. That he still loves us. But love doesn't stop him from living and moving forward, because that's how life moves."

On the way back, we visited our bridge.

We looked for the spot where we'd pitched our tents, but we couldn't tell the exact place. A cool breeze stirred the river as the sun sank down in the sky.

"We should get going," Arul said.

"Just a bit longer," I said. Part of me felt that if you could still talk to me, this was the place where I'd hear your voice loud and clear—here on this bridge, which was the closest we'd had to a happy home.

I whispered your name, again and again, but you never replied.

Or maybe I just didn't hear. All I heard was the river slapping against the bank endlessly.

"It's getting really late," Arul said. "Come on."

Celina Aunty and Muthu were standing in the front yard, peering up and down the street, into the gloom. Muthu waved wildly as soon as he spotted us returning, and Celina Aunty practically ran to the gate to let us in.

"Thank goodness you're here at last, " she said. "What kept you out so long?"

"Told you they'd be fine, Aunty," Muthu said. "Why were you so worried? Because this is the first time Akka and Arul have ever been out on their own in the dark without me, or something?"

"That must be it." She tousled his hair and smiled at us. "But please, next time you want to stay out late, warn me so I don't get scared?"

I promised I would.

And I thought about Celina Aunty and Muthu's concern. It felt good to see them feeling happy that we were back safe.

For the first time since we'd left the bridge, I had the feeling I'd come home.

42

───────◆───────

PAST AND PRESENT

After assembly this morning, Celina Aunty beckoned to me to come see her.

"Surely you can't be in trouble again," Arul whispered.

"You said the prayers today." Muthu rushed to defend me. "I saw. I'll tell them, Akka."

"Thanks, Muthu." I ruffled his hair. "I promise I'll let you know if I need your help."

I followed Celina Aunty into her office.

"Sorry to keep you from your class, but it's your lessons I want to discuss with you." She played with a pen on her desk. "We have a good place here—"

"A great place," I said.

"Glad to hear you say that, Viji. I'm happy to see how you have adjusted. But I've been thinking about where you need to be."

"What do you mean?"

"Our teachers aren't used to teaching children as old as you. Or as good at writing and reading as you are. There are larger schools, where you would have greater opportunities. Better facilities."

"You want me to leave?"

"That's not what I'm saying. This can still be your home, Viji, and you can visit Muthu and the rest of us anytime. But there's a good boarding school where some of our children have gone before. I spoke to the head, and she'd welcome you."

"I haven't said I'll go."

"No." She looked me in the eye. "But if you're serious about teaching at a school someday, you'll need to study a lot more and get much better training than we can give you here. Just think it over, okay?"

It's so strange, Rukku. Just when I start thinking of this as my home, Celina Aunty decides I need to move. On and out of here. I know I need to welcome the chance Celina Aunty is offering me.

Except I don't want to go. You were taken from me, and I'm not ready to take myself away from the two best friends I have left.

Not yet.

———

That evening, Arul and I sat on the bench, watching Muthu chase the little kids, who cackled and screeched. It was good to see him in such high spirits again and to hear him hooting with laughter.

When he came over and joined us, I started telling them about my conversation with Celina Aunty. "She wants to send me to a school—"

"We are at school," Muthu said.

"A bigger school," I said, and explained her offer.

"Super!" Arul thumped me on the back.

"Glad you're so thrilled by the thought of me leaving," I said, watching the kids running about. "But I don't want to go."

"I don't want you to go either," Muthu said. "Stay here, Akka. Never mind what Arul says."

"Don't be silly." Arul's smile left his face, and he got all serious. "She should go. Go and do something she's been dreaming about."

"If I leave, who'd look after Muthu?" I asked.

"I don't need anyone looking after me." Muthu pushed his lip out so far, it looked in danger of falling off his face. "I'll be okay if you go, but I won't like it."

"I won't like it at the other school either," I said. "They'll all probably have nicer dresses. And lots of—"

"You'll always have nicer friends," Arul interrupted. "And nicer family—you'll always have us."

I couldn't argue with that. I put an arm around each of them and drew them closer.

43

◆

OUR FATHER

The next morning I got a visit from our father.

Definitely not the one in heaven.

"How did he know where to find me?" I asked Celina Aunty when she told me he was here to see me. And then the answer came to me. "My letter."

"Probably," Celina Aunty said. "You don't have to see him unless you want to."

"I'll see him," I said.

"Do you want me—or someone else—to stay with you?"

"I'm not scared." If I didn't meet him face-to-face, I'd be afraid he'd try to track me down some other day, when I wasn't in such a safe place. "I'll meet him on my own."

"As you wish." Celina Aunty motioned at the room where he was waiting. "We won't let him take you away by force. But of course, if you decide you want to leave, that's up to you."

Head high, neck maybe a little too stiff, I strode in like a princess. "What do you want?" I said to Appa.

He held out a package, a gift, like he thought it was enough to win me over. I looked at the dark hair sprouting in bushes along his fingers. I could feel his hand coming down across my cheek, whip-fast, leather tough.

"I don't want it," I said. "I don't want anything from you."

His eyes glittered with anger. "You're my daughter," he said. "Mine. I can take the two of you home whether you want to or not."

"You can't," I said. "Not the two of us. Rukku's dead."

"What?" He stared and then whispered, "You're lying."

"No," I said. "I wouldn't lie about something like that!"

A strange sound came from him, a kind of growl that was anger and pain, mixed up. His hand actually trembled. He let the package flop onto Celina Aunty's desk.

Maybe all that Celina Aunty and Arul had said about God and Yesu had made some kind of difference, because all of a sudden, I felt sorry for him, the way he stooped, his arms hanging limp.

On the street, I'd seen dogs fighting. Snarling. Ripping at one another. Until one gave up and tucked its tail between its legs in surrender. That was what Appa reminded me of with his head hanging and his chin almost touching his chest.

Seeing him standing that way, I knew I was larger than he would ever be. For his pitiful sake, I ripped open the package he'd brought. Inside, there were two things. A hand-carved wooden pendant. And a hand-carved doll, just like Marapachi.

"You—you made Rukku a new doll?" I couldn't believe it, but there she was, in my hands, Marapachi's twin. He must have made the old one, too, I realized.

"Yes. I made it for her." He knelt and put his hands together. "Come home. Please. Give me another chance. I'll never, never, never hurt you again."

He shook with sobs, and I put a hand on his shoulder.

Rivers of tears coursed down, crooked, across his cheeks, his stubble-covered chin.

A flash flood of forgiveness rose in my chest. It was a strange kind of forgiveness, mixed with desperate pity and hope. A flood that threatened to drown me if I didn't fight it.

At last, I understood how Amma felt—why she gave in every time he said he was sorry. Understood her eagerness to piece together her shattered image of him. Her need to keep hoping things would get better somehow. She must have felt just as sorry for him as I felt when I saw him kneeling on the ground.

Because at that moment, he truly meant it. He really wanted to be a better man.

I almost did what Amma would have done. I almost gave up the freedom and the future I could have.

That's when I heard your voice, Rukku.

No, you said. *Stay, Viji.*

Your voice was like the beam of a lighthouse, cutting right through my fog of pity.

"No." My voice was calm. My whole body was calm. "This is home now."

"Don't be angry. I'll give you anything, anything—"

"My future is here, Appa."

His knuckles clenched and then unclenched.

"Tell Amma I love her. And don't ever, ever lay a finger on her again."

"Yes." He bowed his head. "And I'll come again to visit you."

"Bring her," I said. "Bring her to visit me."

"I promise," he said.

For the first time in what felt like forever, the touch of his rough hand was gentle on my chin. He held it, held my gaze.

Then he let go and walked out the door, his steps measured, his footfall softened.

I hope he'll keep his promise. But even if he doesn't, his visit left me feeling better.

He took away some of my anger, I think, anger that had been pressing down on my chest. Now that I had let my anger go, it felt like my heart had more room.

———————

After Appa left, I marched up to Celina Aunty, who was waiting anxiously to hear how it all had gone.

"You know that boarding school for girls, the one you wanted to send me to?" I said. "I'll go."

"Yes!" She slammed a fist into her palm. "That's wonderful. You'll be so happy there. I'm so proud of you."

Then the two of us just sat there and smiled and smiled at each other.

At dinner, I told Arul and Muthu about Appa's visit and how much better I'd behaved than I'd ever thought I could.

"There's hope for you yet," Arul said. "Yesu is getting through."

"No," I said. "It was Rukku's voice I heard in my head, not Yesu's."

"Not in your head," Arul said. "You heard her voice in your heart."

Waiting for him to lecture me about you being in heaven, I chewed a mouthful of rice.

But Arul only said, "If you really think the only place Rukku's still alive is inside you, you know what you need to do, right?"

"What?"

"You've got to start loving yourself like you loved her, like you were able to allow yourself to even love your dad."

"Not sure if that was love, exactly," I said. "Anyway, there's something else I need to tell you two."

"What?" Muthu said.

"I'm going to that other school Celina Aunty talked about."

Muthu stuck his tongue out at me, but Arul whooped.

"Yes!" Arul said. "You're going to do so much with your life."

"What if I'm not good enough?" I voiced my fear.

"Then you can come back here," Muthu said. "I hope you're not good enough."

"Don't be silly," Arul said. "She'll become a teacher like she wanted, and she'll build a school for kids like us."

"Who'll you name your school after?" Muthu asked me, as if I were building one already.

"You should name it after our father," Arul said. "Remember? Our father, O. R. T. Narayan. Hallowed be his name."

I was so amazed to hear him joking about God that I said, totally serious, "I'll name it after you, Arul. Rukku and Muthu and you."

"After me?" Muthu grinned. "Then I guess I'd better start paying attention to my lessons."

---◆---

44

WHEREVER YOU ARE

As I write to you now, Rukku, I travel. Back.

I feel the rain on our backs as you crouch on the road, trying to save worms.

I hear you humming to Kutti, holding him close in your comforting arms as a firework explodes on Divali night.

I see your proud smile as you hand the balloon vendor your very own money at the beach.

I see your tongue between your teeth as you concentrate on finishing a bead necklace.

I see your fingertips as you hold the orange the gardener threw at us.

I see you fling your beloved doll at the driver to defend me from danger.

I hear you and Muthu belly laughing together on our bridge.

Your laugh was so strong. So strong it makes me smile, even now, just remembering.

Writing is an odd thing. Writing today, in this book, I realize I sometimes saw things the wrong way around when they were happening.

All this while, I thought I'd looked after you, but now I see it was often the opposite.

You gave me strength.

By never letting me get away with a lie.

By showing me small miracles.

By laughing at all the wrong times.

Together we were such a good team.

And now I'll keep trying, Rukku. To carry your laughter with me and march forward.

To love you but live in today, not in yesterday.

Moving ahead doesn't mean leaving you behind. I finally understand that.

And I guess how you live matters more than how long you live. Every happy moment we had, every bit of love we shared, still glows. We're together in my heart and always will be.

So I'm living with my whole heart, Rukku. And imagining with my whole mind.

Imagining Lalitha, my new friend, all grown up, living on her own, laughing away with Arul and Muthu. Imagining me, all grown up, too, a teacher at last. Imagining you drinking cold, bubbly soda in a nice, fancy palace and burping louder than Muthu ever could.

Imagining you can hear me say, *I love you, Rukku.*

Imagining so hard, I can almost feel you patting me again, see you beaming, hear you saying, *Rukku loves Viji,* right back.

As I was growing up in India, my mother was the only single mom I knew. Despite our own fraught economic situation, she always devoted time and energy to charitable causes—especially those that provided education for children who were even less privileged than I was. Early in my life, I was introduced to the work done by the Concerned for Working Children, an organization that has now grown and become established and been nominated for the Nobel Peace Prize. I also spent time at the village school in Nilbagh, a night school for children of fisherfolk, and a school for Roma children, and I met people involved with organizations such as the Mobile Creches, CRY, and Balbhavan. Even after I moved to the United States, I remained interested in issues confronting children who lack so many of the privileges that I now have. In recent years, along with my mother, my late aunt Visalam, my aunt Renuka, and my uncle Subra, I have had the pleasure of visiting other schools and homes in India where children are offered support and assistance, such as the V-Excel Educational Trust. Celina Aunty's refuge in the book is based on these homes and schools.

Despite all the good work that is done, however, many children face problems that result from a lack of understanding, lack of resources, or lack of compassion. This story draws largely on first-person accounts of what real children have undergone. In writing it, I not only interviewed adults and children but also relied, very heavily, on detailed journal accounts. Many children visited us and confided in my mother, sometimes deeply questioning the existence of a higher power, and I faithfully recorded the tales they told about their struggles in diaries that I kept until I left India in my late teens. Viji's character is modeled in part on a young girl called Indira, who referred to herself as my "akka" and often spent long evenings with my mother, recounting her early life and the terrible trials she had faced. The characters of Rukku, Arul, and Muthu are also based on children I knew, and many of the incidents in the novel are drawn from first-person accounts. Out of respect for the real people on whom this story is based, I felt I could not change fundamental events that took place if I truly wished to honor their memories and their lives.

In India, a staggering number of children—millions—are homeless. In cities, it is commonplace to see homeless children younger than Muthu eking out a living on the streets as best they can. Some children run away because of domestic violence, as Viji does, hoping to find a better life; others are abandoned. Homeless children often face discrimination based on caste, gender, disability, ethnicity, and so on. Many of these children are proud of earning an independent living, and they fight fiercely to hold on to their fragile freedom. A common form of work is sifting through trash to salvage and sell recyclable material; "ragpicker" children may earn less than a dollar a day. And although the exchange rate from dollars to rupees varies, and the cost of articles also fluctuates greatly in India, these children are always paid hardly anything for their work and are forced to live on shockingly little. Unfortunately, these children are in constant danger of being forced into even more terrifying situations; many seek to enslave and abuse them.

Hunger and poverty are not issues that affect South Asia alone. They are global problems that millions of children and adults face. In many parts of the world, children suffer without any end in sight, and without proper food, clothing, housing, and education; they are frequently subjected to violence. As I wrote this novel, I also became increasingly aware of the plight of children in the United States and in my own home state of Rhode Island, where some children still experience problems as basic as hunger and homelessness.

Many children remain strong despite suffering even more severely than the four in this novel, and this book is written with the hope that children everywhere will someday live in a world that treasures and nurtures them.

ACKNOWLEDGMENTS

Thanks to the many who took time out of their busy schedules to speak to me as I conducted research for this novel, as well as the many whom I met as a child (and yes, I was listening and taking notes all those years back, though I didn't let on): Dr. Anadalakshmi, Ms. Amba, Mr. and Mrs. Azaraiah, Dr. Indu Balagopal, Sister Catherine, Ms. Shantha Gandhi, Mr. David Hosburgh, Ms. Rita Kapoor, Ms. Amuktha Appa Rao Mahapatra, Dr. Vasuda Prakash, Ms. Nandana Reddy, and Ms. Mina Swaminathan.

In writing, I elicited the help of several incredible and generous beta readers (doctors, nurses, psychiatrists, psychologists, social workers, teachers, and many people with many diverse backgrounds, some of them writers themselves), among them Lyn Miller-Lachmann, first and foremost; Samuel Stockwell; Cindy Rodriguez; Laurie Rothenberg; Celina Pereira; Amitha Knight; Morgan Goodney; Susan Dubowski; Kristy Dempsey;

Betty Cotter; Carrie Banks; Armin Arethna; Haley; Joanne; the Mutotas and the Bajajs; and the Generations Sangha. Others helped immensely but asked not to be named, and I thank them for their time, attention, and sensitivity.

Profound thanks to my most important readers of all—my brilliant editor, Nancy Paulsen, for her steadfast support of me, unshakable faith in this story, spot-on suggestions, thought-provoking questions, and incredible patience; my agent, Rob Weisbach, for always helping me overcome anxiety and stay cheerful and for providing insightful comments as this story was sculpted into shape; Sara LaFleur, Eileen Kreit, Carmela Iaria, Venessa Carson, Alexis Watts, and the entire team at Penguin Young Readers, who work so hard and with such love and dedication to spread the word about each new book; Jennifer Bricking for the lovely cover; and my husband and daughter, who will, I hope, soon read and love this book (but whom I promise I'll love even if they don't).